VINTAGE **LETTE & CAREY**

Puberty
Blues

VINTAGE **CLASSICS**

Kathy Lette moved on from *Puberty Blues* to work as a newspaper columnist and television sitcom writer in Los Angeles and New York. She has subsequently written eleven international bestsellers including *Girls' Night Out*, *Mad Cows* (the movie starred Joanna Lumley and Anna Friel), *How to Kill Your Husband* (staged by the Victorian Opera), *The Boy Who Fell to Earth* (soon to be a feature film, starring Emily Mortimer) and *To Love, Honour and Betray* (her update on *Puberty Blues*). Her novels are published in fourteen languages. Kathy appears regularly as a guest on the BBC and CNN News. She is an ambassador for Women and Children First, Plan International, the White Ribbon Alliance and the NAS. In 2004 she was the London Savoy Hotel's Writer in Residence, where a cocktail named after her can still be ordered. Kathy is an autodidact (a word she taught herself) but in 2010 received an honorary doctorate from Southampton Solent University.

Kathy lives in London. Visit her website at kathylette.com and on Twitter @KathyLette.

Gabrielle Carey is the author of novels, biography, autobiography, essays, articles and short stories, including *Confessions of a Teenage Celebrity*, about the tumultuous time surrounding the writing and publishing of *Puberty Blues*. For twenty-five years Gabrielle taught writing at various universities including the University of Canberra, the University of Western Sydney and the University of Sydney and the University of Technology Sydney. She is now a full-time writer and vagabond scholar. Her website is gabriellecarey.com.au

KATHY **LETTE**
GABRIELLE **CAREY**

Puberty Blues

VINTAGE **CLASSICS**

VINTAGE

UK | USA | Canada | Ireland | Australia
India | New Zealand | South Africa | China

Vintage is part of the Penguin Random House group of companies
whose addresses can be found at global.penguinrandomhouse.com

Penguin
Random House
Australia

First published by McPhee Gribble, Penguin Books Australia Ltd, in 1979
Published by Text Publishing and Random House in 2012
This edition published by Vintage in 2022

Cover photography: image of car by William Caram/Alamy Stock Photo and Shutterstock;
images of wave and tree courtesy of Shutterstock
Cover design by Louisa Maggio © Penguin Random House Australia Pty Ltd
Internal design by Imogen Stubbs

Printed and bound in Australia by Griffin Press, part of Ovato, an accredited
ISO AS/NZS 14001 Environmental Management Systems printer

A catalogue record for this
book is available from the
NATIONAL LIBRARY OF AUSTRALIA   National Library of Australia

ISBN 978 1 76104 568 4

penguin.com.au

MIX
Paper from
responsible sources
FSC
www.fsc.org   FSC® C009448

CONTENTS

To Virginia Ferguson
our literary godmother

down the beach

WHEN we were thirteen, the coolest things to do were the things your parents wouldn't let you do. Things like have sex, smoke cigarettes, nick off from school, go to the drive-in, take drugs and go to the beach.

The beach was the centre of our world. Rain, snow, hail, a two-hour wait at the bus stop, or being grounded, nothing could keep us from the surf. Us little surfie chicks, chirping our way down on the train. Hundreds of us in little white shirts, short-sleeved jumpers, thongs and straight-legged Levis covering little black bikinis. We flocked to the beach. Cheep. Cheep.

There were three main sections of Cronulla Beach—South Cronulla, North Cronulla and Greenhills. Everyone was trying to make it to Greenhills.

That's where the top surfie gang hung out—the prettiest girls from school and the best surfies on the beach. The bad surfboard riders on their 'L' plates, the Italian family groups and the 'uncool' kids from Bankstown (Bankies), swarmed to South Cronulla—Dickheadland. That's where it all began. We were dickheads.

If you were lucky, your boyfriend would meet you at the station, but usually it was a half-day search through blonde-headed, denim-legged, cigarette-smoking surfboard riders. Searching for *your* Greg. *Your* Wayne. *Your* Bruce. Whoever you happened to be going around with at the time.

I was going around with Greg. I'd met him at South Cronulla. He was my first ever Surfie boyfriend. He couldn't surf but he was better than a Bankie. He may have had a red Coolite, but he'd stuck a fin in it. Sue had her eye on Darryl. He was Greg's best friend. Sue was mine.

Off went the boys into the big, blue sea. Sue and I sat there on the sand. Ten o'clock, eleven o'clock, twelve o'clock…warming up the towel, folding his clothes into neat little piles, fetching the banana fritters and chocolate thick-shakes and watching him chuck endless re-entries.

'Didja see me kneel?'

'Yeah. It was great.'

'I got this really good one and I looked up and *you weren't lookin'!*'

'I was. I saw you. I did.'

2

'Where's the fritters?'

'Here yar.'

By this time Sue and I were starving too but we couldn't eat anything. Skinniness was inniness. Girls never ate in front of their boyfriends. It was unladylike to open your mouth and shove something in it. We were also busting to go to the dunny, but that was too rude for girls. Our stomachs rumbled and our bladders burst. It was a great day at the beach.

Then off they went again, into the big, blue sea, and there we sat. Two o'clock, three o'clock, four o'clock…checking out the guys, sneaking a red ice-block and flirting when I thought Greg wasn't looking.

To pass the time we kept an eyeball peeled for our dreaded enemies—the Bankies, from the greasy western suburbs. They were easy to spot with their yellow T-shirts, Amco jeans, terry-towelling hats, one-piece swimming costumes, worn-out Coolie surfboards and white zinc plastered from ear to ear.

'Oh, I'd wear Amcos for sure.'

'Spot on. Huh! Like ya Coolite!'

'Bankstowner…Er…Pew.'

We gave them heaps.

Finally the sun went down and out came a little blonde, bedraggled, dripping, drowned rat—my boyfriend.

While Greg and Darryl got changed, they sent us off to get their munchies. The art of changing in and out of boardshorts at the beach was always done behind a towel or when your girlfriend was at the shop. The ultimate disgrace for a surfie was to be seen in his scungies. They were too much like underpants. The boys didn't want us checking out the size of their dicks. Greg gorged the meat pie I bought him as we walked up to the station.

'Where's me towel?' he asked, halfway there.

'I haven't got it.'

'Well, I haven't got it! Wait here. Mind this.' He handed me half a sloppy tomato-sauce-sodden meat pie. *'And don't eat it!'*

'Okay.'

Off he ran, thongs flapping, blonde hair flowing.

Then it was a half-hour wait. I was starving. The meat pie was getting cold. There it was in my hot little hand...

'Where's me pie?'

I looked at him blankly.

'Where's me pie?' Sue and I stood speechless. *'You ate it!'* He threw his towel at me. *'You're dropped!'*

Not to worry, he was to drop me ninety-four more times in our relationship.

But in the end, I dropped Greg. He was a rotten surfer. He could only kneel. I decided he was a bit of a Bankie. You didn't have to come from Bankstown to be a Bankie. It just meant anyone who was uncool. Sue dropped Darryl too. We didn't tell them; we just started hanging at North Cronulla.

North Cronulla was north of South Cronulla, and exactly the same really, except the waves were bigger, the boys were older, the shop was closer, the hair was longer and the rank was higher.

We checked out a group of guys sitting on the hill. The Hill Gang. Sue and I walked past a few times and then sat on the rocks nearby. Giggling, we glanced in their direction. I widened my eyes and pouted, trying to look cute. Finally they came over and asked for the time.

Soon I was going round with Mark. He was cooler than the South Cronulla-ites. He had a real Jackson surfboard—with *two* fins on it: a twin fin. Sue had her eye on Warwick. He was Mark's best friend.

Off he went into the deep-blue sea and there I sat on the hill...warming up the towel, folding his clothes into neat little piles, fetching the Chiko rolls and watching him chuck endless cut-backs. When he was a long way out, Sue and I checked out the guys. They were spunkier at North Cronulla. The spunk was thicker and the Bankies fewer.

'There he is!'

It was Darren Peters—the top surfing spunk of the sixth form.

'Where?'

'There! Over there on the wall.'

'Oh Gord. What a doll.'

'Oh, what'll we do? Follow him?'

'No, just sit 'ere.'

5

'Oh no. He's looking!'

'Don't look.'

'Smile!'

'No. He'll think I'm trying to crack onoo him.'

'Oh, there he goes. Oooohhhhh.'

'Oh, he's with that moll. Lucky bitch.'

She was a moll cause she walked everywhere in her bikini. That meant she was showing off her body and was an easy root. You could sit in your bikini but never walk. Spring, summer, autumn, winter, we walked along the beach in Levis, white shirts and thongs.

But then there were the Bankie bikini-wearers.

One day as we sat there on the hill in the blazing hot sun in full dress uniform, a few of our North Cronulla gang started to chuckle. We looked up. There, walking along the beach front, was a tall, skinny, pretzel-looking albino beanpole in a terry-towelling bikini.

'Check out the mohair stockings!'

'I'd walk along the beach with a figure like that for sure.'

She walked along the sand oblivious, leaving a blazing trail of sniggering brown surfies. Her white, hairy body glowed as she loped up the beach.

'Flatsey! Flatsey! You're flat and that's that!' we chorused mockingly.

'Untold zits.'

'Hey ghost features!'

She turned around.

I nudged Sue in horror. It was Judy! Sue's next-door neighbour. We ducked, suddenly fascinated by my right thong. If she saw us we were goners. She'd rush over and say hello. It wasn't cool to know a Bankie chick. We'd be expelled by the Hill Gang and sent back to South Cronulla, in disgrace with our towels between our legs. Back to Dickheadland, where there were millions of Judys, with flat chests, hairy legs and Coolites. Mark saved the day.

'Where's me Chiko roll?' he said, dripping all over us.

We ran all too enthusiastically up the beach in the opposite direction.

Sue and I were trying to make it into the ultimate surfie gang at Greenhills. It was special—the prettiest and coolest girls at school and the best surfers on the beach. Brown and blonde, they stood out in the school playground. The girls were skinny, hair-free, care-free and girlie. They were the shortest uniforms, the most mascara and a friendship ring. Ninety-nine per cent of their time was spent on the roofs of their houses with a bottle of baby oil. For hours they basked, baked and blistered, trying to get browner than Tracey and Cheryl. Sylvania Heights is full of nineteen-year-old girls looking like shrivelled up ninety-year-olds.

The passport into this surfie gang was a brief halter-neck bikini, a pair of straight-legged Levis, a packet of Marlboro cigarettes, a suntan and, if you really wanted to make it, long, blonde hair. To graduate into the surfie gang you had to be desired by one of the surfie boys, tell off a teacher, do the Scotch drawback and know all about sex. You had to be not too fat, but not too skinny. You had to be not too slack, but not too tight. Friendly, but not forward. You had to wear just enough make-up but never overdo it. You had to be interested in surfing, but not interested enough to surf. The surfie girls had a special walk. It was a slow and casual meander. They slouched their shoulders, sunk into their hips and thrust their pelvises forward.

The surfie boys were brown and broad. The longer and blonder the hair, the better. They never wore full school uniform. Their shirts were always hanging out. If they wore school ties, they hung like limp spaghetti round their necks. They never wore underpants but kept their scungies on at all times, always ready to leap into the surf. The better they surfed, the higher their rank. The passport into a surfie gang for boys was a surfboard, a pair of boardshorts, a pair of straight-legged Levis, a packet of Marlboro cigarettes and long, blonde hair. To graduate into the surfie gang you had to have your name called out at assembly, regular canings, and having 'broken in' a couple of young surfie chicks. The surfie boys had a special walk. They bounded along in their rubber thongs, keeping their torsos stiff, sturdy as a lighthouse.

Every school in the southern Sydney suburbs

had a surfie gang—the 'in', cool heavies. They had all the fun. They sneaked down to the creek to kiss and cuddle at lunchtime. They smoked cigarettes. They put eggshells in Mrs Yelland's peanut-butter sandwich. On sunny days they truanted and went to the beach. Then there'd be a big hole in the middle of the quadrangle, at lunchtime, where they usually sat. They had their claimed territory that no one else ventured upon, at school, up the back of the bus and at the beach.

They went out together on Friday and Saturday nights. They got drunk. They had boyfriends and girl-friends. They disobeyed their parents. But the surfie gang had a big, more important family of its own.

The kids who weren't in on the gang spent Friday and Saturday nights at home. They wore flared Amco jeans. They read books. They went to church fellowship and had never heard of Led Zeppelin. If you weren't a surfie chick, you were a nobody. You were a nurd. You could always tell nurds at school. They wore their uniforms longer than ours—two inches over their underpants. They were goody-goodies. They didn't smoke. They were never on detention. Never got their names called out at assembly. They were never in the corridor, never in the headmaster's office and *never* up the back of the bus. But most of all, they didn't have boyfriends. If they *were* 'going round' with anyone, he was bound to have short back and sides, acne and play handball. We thought they were virgin prudes.

Once you made it into the surfie gang, you were a top chick, with a spunky boyfriend. Everyone knew who you were and you knew everyone who mattered.

More than anything, Sue and I wanted to be in the Greenhills Gang. We went through endless packets of Marlboro, practising the drawback. We took up our uniforms. We roasted on the roof all day and rubbed cream into each other all night. If you wanted to get into the gang, you had to crawl after and suck up to all the gang girls. 'Sure! I can lend ya ten cents. Here yar. Have me lunch. Dead-set, I'm not hungry, I just had a curried chop in home science...Geez, you looked priddy on Fridee night at the dance, Kim. Yeah, all the guys were stoked. Should've seen Darren Peters lookin' at ya!...Yeah, reckon, Kerrie's a two-faced bitch. I hate her too.' We lent them our bus fares and walked home, told them how good they looked, offered them cigarettes, agreed with whatever they said and laughed at all their jokes. But nothing worked. We just couldn't get into the Greenhills Gang.

At eight o'clock every morning there'd be a mad rush for the back of the school bus. Everybody had their appointed seat. Every day the same seat next to the same person.

Sue and I raced up the aisle.

'Oh, watch out!' I shrieked, tripping. 'I'd put me bag in the middle of the aisle for sure!'

The smoke was already billowing up from the back of the bus. We sat three seats from the back.

'Gimme a cigarette,' moaned Sue. 'I'm so nervous. I didn't do *any* study. I'm packin' shit.'

'It's cool.' I hitched up my uniform revealing a list of the industrial revolution's consequences between 1850 and 1919. The tops of my thighs were green and blue, covered with facts and dates and names. I handed her a pen.

'Perf!' she said.

I showed off my legs to the girls around me. Gail and Sharon and the other girls from my history class followed suit.

'Hey!' Sue nudged me. 'Here comes Darren.'

'What a deadset doll.'

Darren Peters strode by. He was tall and brown with long blonde hair. Everyone in the aisle parted and the backhangers made room. Darren Peters sat in the very middle of the back seat. The back of the school bus was sacred. It was reserved exclusively for the Greenhills Gang. Cheryl Nolan was already up there, lounging, laughing loudly and flashing her brown thighs. Danny Dixon's hand was darting suspiciously into the folds of her tunic. They flirted, smoked and swore at the first formers and prefects who sat up the very front of the bus in their long uniforms, gloves and hats, reading books. We'd graduated three-quarters of the way down the bus. We hadn't made it all the way yet, but we were determined.

'Pass us a Marlboro, Sue.'

We had regular drawback lessons with Sue's brother but we were still faking it.

'Does it look like I'm doin' the drawback?' I whispered to Sue.

'Blow it out ya nostrils.'

'Give us more room. Move over.'

Sue slid along the seat, her uniform riding up across the tops of her thighs revealing her exam answers. Short uniforms and black underpants were in. Long socks and singlets were out. Everyone checked each other out in PE.

'Didja see Tracey Little?'

'What?'

'In PE. She had love bites all over 'er neck. She told her mother she got hit by a hockey stick.'

'Give us a drag Sue...Who did it?'

'Here yar...Who knows? She never stays with one guy longer than a week.'

'Slackarse.'

'Here she comes.'

Tracey Little was pretty and had a place in the back of the bus. She was a top chick in the Greenhills Gang.

'Ouch!' I screamed. 'Oh rack off!'

'What?' asked Sue.

'Tracey Little just shoved 'er bag inoo me.'

'Stupid bitch.'

Tracey didn't like us moving in on her territory.

As customary, we broke out our oranges, half-peeled them and began to suck. The juices ran down our chins and trickled down our school uniforms.

'Give us a suck,' asked Sue.

If you peeled a whole orange at once, you were a goner. Everyone asked you for a segment.

'K'niver bit?'

'Give us a bite.'

'You owe me some.'

So we all sucked together, saliva, orange juice and cigarette smoke mingling.

'Shit!' I cried. Half an orange had hit me in the head. Tracey Little was up the back of the bus laughing.

'Get up the front were you belong. Ya goody-goody!'

I hurled the rest of my orange right back at her. She stormed up the aisle and shoved me. 'Gutless wonder.' Tracey started pulling me up by the hair. She didn't think I'd stick up for myself but I dug my nails into her long, blonde hair and yanked. We were caught in a headlock, flashing our brief, black hip-nippers at the whole bus.

'What's going on?' boomed the bus driver, pulling on the brake at the uproar. '*Yews can get orf!*' he shouted.

'Ya gunna stop?' I asked, tough but almost in tears. Tracey loosened her grip. We went back to our seats. My head was ringing. The last thing I felt like was an exam.

2

gang girls

THE bell rang. Mr Fairburn directed us in long files from the front to the back of the auditorium. A row of boys. A row of girls. A row of boys. I rushed to sit behind Sue. Cheryl Nolan was behind me. The papers were handed out.

'Keep them face down.'

A deadly hush descended on the hall.

'Thirty seconds to go.'

The air was thick and tense.

'Fifteen seconds to go.'

Mr Fairburn raised his hand, index finger extended towards the ceiling.

'Ten...nine...eyes to the front, Basin...seven... six...five...pens poised...three...two...one...' his arm released like a guillotine. '*Go!*'

There was a rustle of paper and a bowing of heads.

About fifteen minutes into the exam, a few of the girls got itchy legs.

The boys had no easy means of cheating. Jeff Basin, who was sitting across the aisle from me, got stuck on number sixteen.

'Deb...,' he whispered out of motionless lips, 'Hey...Deb. Sixteen?'

I glanced over.

'Sixteen,' he mimed, his eyebrows puckered.

I casually consulted my thigh. The answer was way up under the elastic of my pants. Without answering straight away, I gazed at the ceiling, crossed my legs, chewed my pen as if in thought, glanced at Mr Fairburn, then hissed the answer across the aisle.

'Nineteen twelve.'

Cheryl leant forward to whisper a question. I held up my paper, a little to the right so she could see it. We were all going for it up the back of the hall. Answers were being whispered. Tunics were pulled up. Mr Fairburn was pretty deaf and pretty blind. He was way up the front.

'One more, Deb?' pleaded Jeff.

It was near the end of the exam.

'Forty-six?'

I checked the answer and scribbled it on my rubber. I waited till Mr Fairburn's back was turned. He was pacing up the front aisle saying, 'Five more minutes.' My rubber thudded softly into the aisle between us. Jeff waited a while and retrieved it with his foot. He'd just written down the answer on his paper when his neck was seized in a strangling clamp. A big hairy hand crashed down on his desk. It was the deputy head.

'Hand it over, Basin.'

He gulped and tried to wiggle out of Mr Berkoff's grasp. Berkoff hauled him up by the neck. 'Get to the office boy!' he said. He turned and began to tap the other culprits on the head with his Bic biro. 'And you, you girls—Susan Knight, Deborah Vickers. Headmaster's office, right this minute. Pronto.'

Sue and I slunk out to the quadrangle for lunch. The Greenhills Gang were on their usual seats in the sun.

'Debbie! Sue!' Cheryl called out to us. 'Come here! What'd Bishop say? Did he go off?' she asked us.

'Oh, yeah.' I shrugged coolly.

'Is he gunna send a letter home to ya olds?'

'S'pose.'

'So he craked 'eh? Didja dob?'

'On you?…No way.'

Cheryl smiled and nodded to the others and even Tracey Little looked approving. Dobbing was the weakest act anyone could pull. The gang girls gathered around to put us to the final test. We may have failed our history exam, but this exam was far more important.

'What's a sixty-niner?' Cheryl interrogated.

'Oh…you know,' Sue said, glancing nervously at the listening boys.

'What then?'

'Head to tail.'

'What does buckin' mean?' asked Kim Cox.

I demonstrated, jerking my pelvis backwards and forwards. Susan followed suit. The boys guffawed crudely.

Tracey looked us up and down. 'Comin' down the dunnies for a fag?'

She led the way. Kim kept guard at the door of the girls' toilets. The rest of us disappeared into separate cubicles. We closed the toilet lids and stood up on them. Our heads emerged over the top of the adjoining walls and, as usual, the first formers pulled up their pants and rushed out of the toilet block, screaming.

'Here yar.' Cheryl dealt out the cigarettes. We lit up. I dragged back and swallowed a huge gulp of smoke, held on to it for a few seconds and then blew two professional looking ribbons of smoke from my nostrils. Feeling confident, I manoeuvred my mouth into my smoke-ring position, but they hatched in furry, fluffy blots.

'Oh, handle it, Debbie,' Cheryl sneered, blowing three perfect rings from large to small, with the smallest sailing elegantly through the larger ones.

'Deadset!' said Sue.

'Perf!'

Kim's head shot round the toilet door. 'It's Yelland! Quick!' Our heads bobbed down and the toilets flushed simultaneously. The other girls sauntered out.

'Meetcha up the back of the bus this arvo,' Tracey

hissed to Sue. I pulled the chain again and again, but the cigarette butt floated obstinately in the toilet pool. I stuffed my mouth with peppermint Lifesavers and walked out as casually as I could. The girls' counsellor was standing there.

'Eating in the toilets, Deborah?' Mrs Yelland eyed me suspiciously. 'You're cultivating bad habits.'

That afternoon we'd made it. We were sitting up the back of the bus—sucking oranges, doing the drawback and knocking the kids who sat up the front. We were tough. We were accepted. We were part of the sacred set.

'K'niver drag Darren?'

Once we were admitted into the gang by Tracey and Cheryl and the rest of the girls, they arranged a match for us with two of the boys.

'He'll roolly suit ya.'

'Yeah, you'll look roolly good together.'

The best thing about being in the gang, was that all the spunkiest guys on Cronulla Beach were in it. It didn't matter what boy picked you, 'cause in the looks department, you never got a bummer.

3

a roolly good couple

'BRUCE Board likes you.'

'I've never seen 'im but.'

'He's seen you.' Kim had cornered me in the canteen.

'You'll like 'im. You really will Debbie.'

'What does he look like?'

'He's got long blonde hair,' said Kim, sinking her teeth into a cream doughnut and spraying icing sugar all over both of us.

'But does he like me?'

'Yeah. You'll make a roolly good couple.'

'Who told you but?'

'I can't tell ya…but believe me.'

'Yeah, but what if he doesn't like me?'

'He does. Ask Tracey. *Trace!*'

Tracey sauntered across the canteen. She had long

blonde hair, a good figure and a top boyfriend. She was pretty, but she was tough.

'Want a bite?' I asked, eagerly extending my finger bun—a long, thick, usually stale bun with a strip of pink icing.

'Thanks.' Tracey took a huge bite and opened up the bun.

'Oh, mint of the margarine. Check out how much they give ya.'

She displayed two measly dabs of margarine inside the slobbery yellow bun.

'Scabs,' I agreed.

'She won't believe me,' said Kim.

'I *do!*'

'Wot?' asked Tracey.

'That Bruce Board likes her.'

Tracey turned on me seriously. 'He does,' she said, her mouth full of pineapple doughnut. 'Look, we've arranged it.'

'What?'

'Be down the paddock this Friday afternoon.'

'Why?'

'Bruce wants to meetcha.'

'But what if he doesn't like m…' *Bbbbrrring*. It was the end of lunchtime. Masses of kids full of cream buns and Coca-Cola began to move out of the canteen into the quadrangle. Tracey, Kim and I stuffed our used cake wrappers into the bubbler and gave the drink machine a kick.

Jeff Basin rushed over. 'Lend us three cents will ya?'

'Nu. Haven't got none. Comin' down the paddock on Friday?' asked Tracey.

'Bloody oaf. Gunna meet Boardie, Debbie?...Ha, ha, ha, ha...'

Friday morning I packed black, straight-legged Levis and blue jumper into my school bag. I buried a packet of Marlboro in the depths of my bag and went to school. I was packin' shit all day.

'What'll I say but?'

'You'll be all right.'

'What if he doesn't like me?'

'Oh, shut up.'

I changed in the back of the bus, dodging cigarettes and airborne orange peels. I pulled my jeans up under my uniform. I left on my white school shirt, tucked it in and pulled the tunic over my head. The bus driver grinned at me in the rear-vision mirror.

'Lend us ya brush Sue.'

'Here ya.'

Sue had changed into straight-legged Levis and a green jumper.

Tracey, Sue and I got off at Waratah Street and made the trek to the paddock.

'Do I look all right?' I kept saying.

We walked past Kim's place. Her elder brother Danny was out the front washing the car. He checked us out as we walked past.

'Hey, Debbie?' he called.

'Hi Danny.'

'Come here.' I went over. 'Is that Susan Knight?' he said, eyeing Sue up and down.

'Yeah.'

'Is she goin' round wiv anyone?'

'Oh…um…ah…No.' They were both short with long blonde hair and would make a good couple.

'Yews goin' down the paddock?'

'Yeah.'

'See yas there later.'

We walked off down the highway.

'He likes you Sue.'

'He does not.'

'He *does*.'

'How would you know?'

'He wants to know if you're going' roun' wiv anyone.'

'I don't like him. I'm goin' roun' wiv Wazza anyway.'

'Sue!' I shrieked in disgust. 'Drop Waz! Danny can surf almost as good as Deakin. Don't you know?'

The flame trees in the paddock were swaying and tossing. It was a cold and windy afternoon. The whole gang was waiting for us—Dave Deakin, Wayne Wright, Seagull, Johnno, Glen Jackson, Steve Strachan and Hen. All the girls were on their horses.

'Ah, Kim's a good bucker!' cried Steve Strachan as Kim rode Cochise into the scene. The boys sniggered and nudged one another. It was well known a girl was a better root if she rode a horse.

Everyone checked us out as we walked across the paddock. We'd learnt the special walk—small swivel of the bum, head hanging, hands glued to sides and a terribly casual bounce.

'That's him over there,' whispered Tracey. Bruce Board was tall, blonde and drove a panel van. He'd left school early, like some of the boys in the gang. He was a top guy 'cause he had money, a car and a brand-new board. Now all he needed was a brand-new chick.

Bruce and I sauntered towards each other. The gang circled the chosen two, jeering and prodding.

'Go get 'er Brew.'

'Kiss 'er Boardie. Go on.' The ring closed in around us. My heart was thumping.

'Come on…We're waitin'…'

'Rip in Brew. Don't be shy…' Sneer, snigger.

This was it. He took me by the shoulders and we kissed.

'*Yyaaaay.*'

'Ooooooh. Woo.' Whistle.

'We're goin' for a walk,' he told me, leading me off to the bushes by the hand.

'It only takes ten minutes,' called out Strack after us. The boys roared with laughter.

Behind the lantana we kissed again.

'Will you go round wiv me?' he said.

And that was the courting ceremony in Sylvania Heights, where I grew up. Everyone was 'going around' with somebody. If a guy didn't have a girl-friend, he'd just pick one from a distance. Someone about his height, his hair colour, not too fat, not too skinny and always wearing a pair of straight-legged Levis. Danny picked Sue that way.

You didn't necessarily have to like a guy to go out with him. If he was part of the gang and he chose you, you felt privileged. You'd go out with him about three times...well, you wouldn't actually go out with *him*. You'd go out with his gang to a party and when everyone else paired off, he'd lead you outside for a pash on the front fence, or a 'finger' behind the Holden, or a 'tit-off' down the other end of the hall nearly in the linen press. You wouldn't talk, you'd just 'be with' him. From that night on, you'd know you were going around with him.

At South Cronulla we'd let the boys 'tit-us-off' and occasionally get a hand down our pants. At North Cronulla we'd progressed to dry roots. When we graduated to our new gang at Greenhills, we'd hit the big time. It was time for the spreading of the legs and the splitting up the middle.

You had to 'go out' with a guy for at least two weeks before you'd let him screw you. You had to time it perfectly. If you waited too long you were a tight-arsed prickteaser. If you let him too early, you were a slack-arsed moll. So, after a few weeks, he'd ask you for a root, and if you wanted to keep him, you'd do it.

26

4

that's the way it goes for girls

I was thirteen.

I'd been out of primary school a year.

It was in the back of a panel van.

I hadn't even got my periods yet.

I didn't even know where my hole was.

Actually, I thought there was only one hole, for pissing and having sex.

I tried to find out about it at school that day. I couldn't ask Sue 'cause she knew as much as me. I asked Tracey and Cheryl and the gang. I hadn't learnt that girls don't talk about doing it.

'What am I s'posed to do?'

'Just lay back. He'll know what he's doin'.'

He'd kissed me the first night. Titted-me-off the second night. And fingered me the next night. I bluffed it for a few days... 'Oh, I'm on m' rags.' But it was my duty on Friday night at the drive-in, to go all the way. I counted the hours to my initiation.

'Six…seven…eight hours to go…I'm packin' shit.'

'Look, you've used a Med, haven't you?' Tracey reassured me.

'No.'

A flicker of concern crossed her face. 'Oh. You'll be all right.'

There were six of us in the panel van. I sat in the front, calmly smoking a cigarette, listening to the suppressed screams of agony as Sue lost her virginity to Danny in the back.

That's the way it goes for girls. Every car in the parking lot was doing it…rocking up and down to the panel-van bop. Then it was my turn. I couldn't say no. Bruce had picked me out of all the other girls. Bruce was the top guy of the gang. Even better than Darren Peters. He was the eldest. He had a car, a job, money and the biggest prick.

He parted the purple curtains his mother had made for him, and pulled me over the seat. We undressed in silence, hauling off our jumpers and straight-legged Levis. I stretched out on the pink mattress. The windows began to fog.

He had a little tin in the back of the panel van, that everyone called the 'Tool Kit'—full of frenchies. He used one with me.

After much fumbling…'Ah…' A groan of satisfaction. 'Now I'm gettin' somewhere.'

'That's my bum hole,' I whispered, embarrassed.

I produced the jar of vaseline he'd asked me to bring. Things got mighty slippery…but it still hurt. I thought I was going to pass out.

He grunted and pushed harder. I clutched on to his hips.

'Stop squeezin' m' hips.' I pressed my feet up against the back of the seat. He groped around for my breast. It was so small he couldn't find it.

After a while he gave up. I didn't know whether it'd worked or not. I didn't know what it was supposed to feel like.

I don't remember what happened next. We were just putting on our clothes…strapping myself into a bra that was holding up air.

'I can't find my underpants.' I fumbled around and put everything on inside out. We climbed into the front as Kim and Dave got in the back. 'K'niver cigarette?' I asked.

And that was the initiation in the Greenhills gang. That's the way every girl in the gang lost her virginity. The boys had to be good surfers and the girls had to be good screws.

Well, at least I was doing something on Saturday nights.

5

top guys

BEING with the boys made me feel important. They had a 'thing' in life. Sort of like a religion. And they were devout. They went anywhere, in any kind of weather to any kind of surf. And we trotted along to entertain them when the sun went down. We went to any lengths to be with them. We'd sneak out of bedroom windows. Truant, Lie. Run away from home. Walk down to the beach in the pouring rain or sit on the sandhills in the blazing sun from dawn to dusk to watch their flick-outs and drop-ins. We'd go to the drive-in and come home three hours late when we knew our mothers would have rung up all the neighbours and the police and would be sitting up, waiting, with the feather duster.

It didn't matter what the consequences were 'cause if you were with the surfers you felt as though you were *doing* something. The surf really mattered. Surfing was immortal and everything else was secondary. During the day they were just a bunch of black specks paddling out to sea. The only time we had any chance of getting any affection or attention was at night when it was too dark to check out the tubes. Then he'd rip into you. He'd be sun-soaked, salty, strong, soft and warm. Sometimes you'd think it was all worth it. But next day you may as well have been a baked dinner that he'd gorged, enjoyed and forgotten.

The next day he'd be back down the Point, checking out the southerly swells and right-handers.

The beach was the most sacred place of all. Boys' boards came before everything. It was waves, then babes. They were faithful to the sea and we were faithful to them.

Sue and I had learnt the rules and at last made it to Greenhills. It was about an hour's walk up the endless beach.

We spotted our gang. Sue and I mosied along, really cool.

'Hi, Danny.'

'Hi, Bruce.'

We dropped our towels and collapsed. There was Strack, the Brown-Eye chucker. Gull, short for Seagull. He could stay in the water longest. Wayne Wright, Cheryl's boyfriend. Tall, spunky, top-sufer, Dave Deakin. Glen Jackson, the doll, Johnno, Hen, a few others and Danny and Bruce, our boyfriends.

Soon the other girls arrived, galloping up the beach on their frothing horses. There was Kim on Cochise, Tracey on Rebel, Vicki on Prince, Cheryl on Randy and Kerrie on Candy.

Kerrie got conned into holding the horses while we had a cigarette break. Pulling out our Marlboros, we had smoke-ring competitions and flirted. The girls mounted up and galloped off along the beach. The boys mounted up and dived in. Sue and I were left behind. My horse, Misty, had gone lame. Sue didn't have one but we always doubled. Now we couldn't ride for a month.

It sure was boring sitting alone on the beach.

'Oh, Bruce, lend us ya board,' I begged, squeezing my little boobies together with folded arms. They pouted out my black stocking-lined, crocheted-by-Auntie-Janet, bikini top.

'Go ask Johnno.'

'Oh, Johnno, lend us ya—'

'Bite ya bum.'

Susan began to pester Danny.

'Go on Danny. It's not fair.'

'Go ask those other guys up the beach,' he said, pointing to a bunch of black specks. We made the trek to another tribe.

'Can two of you lend us your boards?'

They looked at us dumbfounded. Then the tallest, brownest, blonde-hairedest spoke up.

'Watja want me board for?'

'For a ride.'

'Oh hand roun'—you'll ding it.'

'Where yas come from?'

'How old are yas?'

'What do ya want a board for?'

It was no use.

After two weekends of hassling we finally got the boards for half an hour as the surf was flat. The other gang guys had gone to catch the afternoon swell at Sandshoes.

Vicki, Greg Hennesey's chick, came with us. We hauled on the boys' boardshorts, giggling and squealing.

'Oh, they're too big.'

'How do you do up this fly, Danny?'

'Bruce, will you do up mine?'

'Oh, they keep falling down. Hee, hee, hee...'

'Hope we don't get a board rash.'

'At least we won't get jungle rash*,' whispered Vicki.

With our boards under our arms, and our boardshorts flapping, we trotted down to the shore-breakers.

We paddled three feet out into the seething two-inch swell. Vicki nose-dived. I slid off. Sue made it to shore. Out we paddled again. Vicki nose-dived. I slid off, and Sue kneeled for a fraction of a second. After catching two waves we were exhausted. We lay on our boards and let the surf take us to shore. There we

---

*Itching and chafing of the testicles from wet boardshorts.

stretched out on our waxy mattresses, panting.

'*Oh no!*' I gasped, clutching my board. 'Don't look now.'

We all looked. No. It couldn't be. It wasn't possible. But there he was. He was supposed to be round at Sandshoes.

'Darren Peters!' Vicki and Susan shrieked in unison.

'What'll we do?'

'And Glen Jackson too.'

'Just lay here.'

'Don't look.'

'Smile.'

'He saw us.'

Darren was the King of Cronulla Beach. Tough. Cool. Sexy. Brown. Strong. Where Darren Peters walked, Dickheads feared to tread.

We were to talk about this for weeks.

'…and then Darren Peters walked up the beach.'

'What? *Darren Peters?*'

'Yeah. He saw us surfin'. Oh God, it was just so embarrassing.'

We got out straight away, pulled up our board-shorts and staggered back to our boyfriends. They laughed at us zig-zagging towards them, too weak to carry the boards against the wind. They checked their boards for dings and stood over us as we waxed them. I'd watched them often enough to know what to do. We pulled on our tight Levis over sandy, dripping crocheted costume pants.

35

The gang boys had hauled tyres from the local Sandhills tip. The girls arrived on their horses. Black smoke belched into the sky as we huddled around to keep warm. The fire raged and Cronulla knew the Greenhills Gang were going. Then the storm clouds came and it was a mad race up the beach that we never won.

By horse, train or car, we made our way home, all sandy, soaked and exhausted. Sue and I picked off the last grains of sand from our jeans pockets, hair and toenails.

'Oh yeah, Mum, the pictures were great...'

Each different surfing gang up and down the south coast has its own rules which you must respect when surfing in their territory. Each group resents the intrusion of any other tribe on to their beach. Cronulla surfies wage an endless war against the kids who come from the Western Suburbs. They're called Bankies, Towners or Billies. Cronulla being at the end of the train line, all sorts of tattooed, greasy, bad-surfing undesirables slide off. Boys from Cronulla are just as unwelcome on other beaches. For instance when you're surfing inside a tube, you call out 'Ooh!' so the other boys know not to 'drop in' on you. When Bruce did this at Wattamolla* Beach, three touch locals approached him later. 'You don't say, "Ooh", 'ere mate,

*Running joke: 'What-a-moll-ah?'

36

you say, "Ay!" Why doncha go back to where ya come from? We don't want any Cronullaites round 'ere.'

When the surf's been especially bad for a few weeks, one surfie gang I know reckons they can get the waves pumping again. They get a dinged-up old board that's going mouldy out the back and strip it. A stake is plunged into its centre as a mast. A pair of scungies, which last about as long as a board, are strung up as a sail. Now it's time for the sacrifice. Girls are forbidden to attend. The board is set alight and cast out to sea. This pleases the God of the Seas, King Huey, named after a great ex-surfer. The next day, so the boys tell me, it's perfect tubes and nine-foot swells.

Another ritual is the surfie funeral service. Once when a local top-surfer was drowned in freakish big seas, for three days after no one was allowed into the water. The locals guarded the beach. They were paying their respects to the dead. Sanden Point went unsurfed as the perfect tubes rolled in.

The customs differ slightly from beach to beach. Dave Deakin, one of our top guys in the gang, moved from Cronulla up to Coolangatta a few years ago. He died there soon after from a heroin overdose. Nearly every surfie in Cronulla paddled out, past the point, to sit in half an hour's silence, mourning the death of their best surfer. One guy hurtled his board off the top of Cronulla Point where it smashed on the rugged rocks below.

Susan and I had our own little ritual. When sitting on the beach every weekend in the rain, hail or blistering, burning, thousand-degree heatwave got too boring, we tried staying home. We filled out *Dolly* quizzes, watched TV and waited and waited for the boys to show up. When that boredom became unbearable, Sue and I did rain dances on the verandah. We 'whooped' and 'stomped' and made genuine Daniel Boone Indian war cries round and round a beach towel. If the boys had seen us we would have been dropped. It never worked anyway. The sun still shone and the boys still surfed. We only ever saw them when the waves and the sun went down. Somehow, we had to get their attention. The gang girls stopped going to the beach on Saturday. We took up our own sport.

Saturday morning, after a breakfast of Cornflakes and sugar, all of us girls made our way to jazz ballet. On the way we called at the cake shop for a quick cream bun or a custard tart.

There was Tracey, the doll, Kim, Danny's sister, giggly Vicki Russell and Cheryl with the bow legs. Everyone knew she was a moll; you could tell by the way she walked. She wasn't a gang-bang moll though. The boys liked her and she didn't root for nothing. She always got a friendship ring. Then there was Kerrie who was on the fringe of the gang. She was going round with Gull but he was only using her. And Sue and me.

We lined up in our tight leotards and little terry-towelling shorts, not quite covering our coloured underpants. Black undies were only for school. Every time we bent over, there'd be flashes of red, yellow, pink, lace, spots, leopard-skin...but never cottontails. Only nurds wore them. We practised a dance over and over to T-Rex. We were all desperately jealous of Kim who had the star role. She had a disjointed hip which she could flick out impishly. Sue and I stood at the very back waving our arms like fleshy windscreen wipers. Bronwyn was the teacher. She went on Bandstand *and* she was engaged!

'Debbie and Susan stop talking or I'll send you out!'

For fifty cents each, it was one and a half hours of torture. The room was a mass of half-shaven legs, pointed toes, bottom cheeks peeping out, thighs, long swinging hair, giggles and groans.

After class we ran up Waratah Street, past Glen Jackson's house, all screaming and giggling, hoping Glen wouldn't see us in our shorts. Most of us wished he would though. First it was a banana and sugar sandwich at Kim's. That killed about an hour. Then it was a GI cordial drink at my place and maybe a biscuit. We talked about the boys.

'Deadset Kim, Dave's stoked in you.'

'Yeah, he told Bruce down the pub that he just wouldn't look at another chick.'

'Oh, you'll be goin' roun' together for heaps. Danny reckons Dave's getting' ya a ring for ya birthday.'

Finally we tropped up to Sue's place to play ping-pong. Not to feel idle, we practised jazz ballet and worked up few of our own routines. We pretended we were going to show them off to the boys. Kim flicked her hip, Vicki giggled, Cheryl shouted and flashed her friendship rings. Tracey looked pretty, Sue and I cracked jokes and Kerrie didn't do anything.

One afternoon our rain dance worked. The surf dropped off. Mrs Knight let the boys in and disappeared to the kitchen. A series of jeans filed down the spiral staircase into the rumpus room. Denim Levis. Cord Levis. Green Levis. Black Levis. Patched Levis. *Never* Amco and *never* flared. And there was blonde hair—long, blonde, sun-bleached, stiff, straw-like, damp, salty, straight-from-the-sea hair. The girls were so brushed and the boys were so rugged.

We giggled and pranced about, pretending to be embarrassed in our shorts. All afternoon we showed off and bent over. They still didn't notice us.

'Dropped in on Towner today.'

'Oh good onya mate.'

'Yeah, he was a roole egg.'

'Didja see the tubes this morning?...Perf!'

'Wanda was pumpin!'

'Bummer it dropped off.'

'Shouda seen me in this unroole tube, eh Deak?'

The boys pulled out their Marlboro cigarettes. Us girls hovered around them, listening attentively.

'Oh didja Danny?'

'Gee you're brave Bruce.'

'K'niver fag Glen?'

For the rest of the afternoon, the boys took turns at the ping-pong table, shouted at each other and smoked cigarettes. The girls smiled, bludged smokes and looked attractively bored.

It was fantastic to have the boys for a whole afternoon.

6

he led you in by the hand

ON Saturday evening, we girls got ready. Little bit of blusher, black mascara, blue eye-shadow and perfume. Only a few of us could afford make-up *and* cigarettes out of our pocket money so the rest of us stole it from our local chemist. We wore straight-legged Levis, casual suede shoes, little white shirts, jumpers and zipped coats. It was a comfortable uniform.

We usually met at Sue's place, even when her parents were home, because there was a little TV room downstairs. The whole gang crammed in. There was some stupid show on that none of us were really watching. It was just an excuse to sit or lie next to the person you were vaguely interested in. If you didn't have too many pimples he'd probably be vaguely interested back. Within an hour, all the couples would be snuggled up and smooching anywhere they could fit.

Over the night-and-day, under the night-and-day, in between the goldfish tank and the piano, draped across the television aerial, under and across the ping-pong table or compressed together like two bits of corned beef in a vinyl armchair sandwich.

You'd always just get comfortable and Mrs Knight would come down to bring us a packet of chips. The sound of her scuffs clapping on the stairs went through us like an electric shock. By the time she got down to the bottom of the stairs, we were brushed, buttoned, zippered, upright, legs crossed and sitting at attention.

'What's on the telly?' she asked. Our blank faces turned up to her.

'Um...'

'Oh...well...It's been good, really good...hasn't it...Danny?'

'Mmmmmmm...bin a lot of ads but...'

'Well I'm off now dears.' Sue's was the best place to hang, 'cause Mr and Mrs Knight were always going to the club. 'There's plenty of soft drink in the fridge and I've left out some lamingtons and Cheezels so look after your guests, Susan. I've left the number of the club by the phone. Behave yourselves now.'

As soon as the Ford turned out of the driveway, the boys leapt into violent games of ping-pong, shouting at each other, smoking cigarettes and frisbeeing the ping-pong bats. Us girls sat in terror of the little room. This was an adjoining spare bedroom, supposed to be used as a study.

At any time of the night, you could look up and notice one couple missing: Johnno and Tracey, Sue and Danny, Dave and Kim, Garry and Vicki, Gull and Kerrie or Cheryl and her current—either Wayne, Glen Jackson or Darren Peters. It was like musical screws. Somehow or other, at some time of the night, you found yourself conveniently positioned near the door of the little room. When the coast was clear, he led you in by the hand. Your boyfriend wedged the Coolite surfboard under the door handle and against the wall like a foam burglar alarm.

Bruce was still trying to screw me. We both took off our clothes. I could see this great, hulking, looming thing in the darkness, with blonde hair and glasses. Then there was a hand on my breast. Knead. Knead. Knead. Not that I had much breast. I had developed certain positions to make my boobs seem bigger. There was the lying-on-my-side-crunching-them-together-with-my-arms position. There was the bending-over-letting-them-hang position...because when I lay down on my back, they seemed to disappear.

I didn't know how he got an erection. I didn't even know what an erection was. There was just this hard, mysterious thing zooming towards me as Bruce mounted and shoved it in. Well, he tried to shove it in. He tried and tried and tried to shove it in. For half an hour he tried.

'We need some Vaseline.' He broke the painful silence.

I had to put all my clothes back on; orange hip-nipper underpants, little white shirt, zippered coat, shoes and socks. I smoothed down my hair, climbed over the Coolite and left the little room...alone.

Vaseline was an essential in surfie-life. It was used to soften eyebrows before plucking, rub into surf-board rashes, pull off your randy horse and various other things.

Everybody watched me as I crossed the room and went up the spiral staircase. I searched everywhere; in bathroom cupboards and dressing tables. Down I went again.

'Where's the vaseline?' I whispered to Sue.

'In the bathroom drawer.'

Now the whole gang knew why I was going back-wards and forwards across the room like a ping-pong ball.

When I returned Bruce was waiting naked and patiently. I pulled the Vaseline out from my under-pants, handed it to the Maestro and undressed in the darkness.

Things got gooey. He drowned me in petroleum jelly and coated himself. He mounted me and tried again. He tried and tried and tried to shove it in. It just wouldn't work. What a marvellous sensation! Being split up the middle!

'Stop 'angin' onoo me 'ips.'

I let go and clutched the bedspread, digging in my fingernails. I waited in agony to pass out.

He gave up.

We dressed in silence, dismantled the surfboard security system and it was Tracey and Johnno's turn.

I've still got that rusty little jar of Vaseline, all these years later, full of eyebrow and pubic hair. A little something to remember my first love.

And that was our Saturday night. It never much varied. It was either a night in the back of the panel van at the drive-in, hanging someone's place when their parents were out or gate-crashing a party.

7

rugged stuff

BRRING…BRRRINGG…

'Susan! Telephone.'

'Who is it?' she called up the stairs.

'It's Danny.'

'Okay.' She raced up the stairs to the lounge.

'Hi Danny.'

'Hi.'

'How are ya?'

'Not too bad.'

'Oh…how was school?'

'Ah, not too bad.'

'Oh…It was really funny in history today. Debbie and I were just sittin' there and Mr Nashville walked in, oh God, and he—'

'Hang on.' *Clunk.* Sue could hear the television in the background. It was Thursday night, the *Benny*

Hill Show. Danny wouldn't miss it for the world. Five minutes later he returned to the receiver.

'Danny, wadaya doin'?'

Chuckle, chuckle. 'Oh God, he's just so funny. Should've seen what he just did...'

'Who?'

'*Benny Hill!* This chick was just walkin' across, and her pants fell down ha ha ha, and she fell over, and Benny Hill went up to her and ha ha ha...hang on, the ads are over.' *Clunk.*

Sue clutched the receiver and stared at the ceiling. And it was a five-minute wait till the next break. She heard the music for the Lemon Fab ad, and braced herself. Danny related the last ten minutes of the show. He told her about Benny standing up and Benny sitting down. Benny running. Benny falling over. Susan laughed in all the right places.

'Danny,' she interrupted, 'what are we doin' tomorrow night?'

'...and then he took this chick and...'

'Danny!'

'Huh?'

'What are we doin' on Fridee night?'

'I dunno. What do you wanna do?'

'Well I dunno. Tracey's parents are goin' out.'

'Who told ya?'

'Vicki.'

'Who's goin'?'

'I dunno. Boardie, Johnno, Cheryl and everyone...'

'Oh…righto, I'll ring Boardie. He can pick us up. Hang on, the ads are over…' *Clunk.*

Everybody was there. Tracey had invited her five best friends and it had ended up with the Greenhills Gang, the Woolooware boys and every surfie between the Bowling Alley and Cronulla Point. The backyard was thick with kids. All in straight-legged Levis and thongs. All swaggering around with bottles of beer and Brandivino. Steven Strachan was there…*the* Sylvania heavy. He raped chicks regularly under the bowling alley, and bragged about it.

'What about Frieda Cummins?…ha ha ha…'

I pricked up my ears for gossip.

'Small gang-bang 'eh,' he said sarcastically. Chuckle, chuckle. 'Nelly come out 'er mowf.'

'What a slack-arsed moll,' I whispered to Sue.

'But do ya reckon she liked it?' Sue ventured.

'I dunno!' Gull laughed, gulping down some more beer. 'Neva asked 'er.'

'*She loves it,*' cried Steve Strachan sucking on his bottle, swaying in Sue's direction. Sue stepped back. Steve Strachan was the heavy of the Greenhills gang. He was six feet tall, wore ugg boots, a lumber jacket, a big, black moustache, and his teeth, when he sniggered, were like fangs. He fingered girls in the pub pool. When he jumped in, everyone jumped out.

'Yeah, twenty of us went frew 'er,' Steve boasted. 'She loved it.'

'She kept fallin' asleep but,' Gull complained.

'Oh, ya jest gotta slap 'er round a bit. Roll 'er over. Stick it in. Twist it roun'. Haul it out…(snigger, snigger) she loved it.'

Molls made me feel sick. How could anyone love it?

'Yeah, she sucks a mean cock,' Strack slobbered. 'Don't hog the bottle Gull!'

'Hey Susie,' I whispered, 'there's Cheryl.'

Cheryl was staggering around the yard, falling all over the boys.

'Oooh'ar, she's drunk.'

'Hope Wayne doesn't find out….'

'She's gonna get a bad name.'

'And she got a ring from him last week…What a moll…Oh, gidday Cheryl.'

Her big mouth dropped open, 'Hi.'

Gull turned around. 'Oh, it's Noaln. Watcha bin drinkin' Nolan?' He looked at the bottle she was grasping. 'Tequila…rugged stuff for a little girl.'

'Oh shuddup,' she drooled.

We gasped. Nobody ever told Gull to shut up.

'What? You drunk little girl? You'd better drink some milk. Wait here.'

Gull returned with a glass of milk from the kitchen.

'Drink this,' he ordered, handing it to Cheryl. She looked at it in disgust. She looked at him in disgust. She looked back at the glass. *Splat!*

Oh my God. Milk all over Seagull.

Sue and I drew back into the shrubs and considered leaving.

Gull sobered, drew himself up and growled.

Suddenly from the balcony came a shout: 'Tracey's olds are home!'

A mass of drunken teenagers swarmed over the back fence and down the side, throwing their cans over with them. Gull hauled Cheryl over and in three seconds the yard was clear and the lights in the house were turned off.

'Susie, is that you?' I whispered from behind the barbecue.

'Yeah.'

'Let's get out of here.' We sneaked down the side passage and met the boys at Boardie's panel van.

'Sprung!' cried Jeff Basin, the local dubbo.*

'Oh der,' moaned Boardie sarcastically. 'Come on, let's split.'

'Reckon.' I sat next to Bruce in the front seat, my hand on his thigh. Danny pulled Sue over the back. He stank of stale beer and cigarettes.

'Come on…' he slobbered, mauling her breast. He hadn't got a screw since last weekend.

She lay down in silence and started peeling off her Levis, zippered coat and little white shirt as we bounced along the road.

Halfway up the Princes Highway, Bruce hit the brakes.

*Idiot/Bankie-type.

53

'Hey. There's Jacko! Get in Jacko! Jump in the back!'

So Glen Jackson jumped in the back, just in time to see Susie madly pulling on her leopard-skin underpants.

She was terrified. Jacko had a big mouth. Now she'd be known as a moll. The whole of Sylvania would know. It'd be scratched into school desks... whispered about behind her back in the canteen...

'Small swell today, eh Danny?'

'Yes, nor' east badly, Jack.'

'Reckon. Gidday, Susan.'

Maybe he hadn't noticed after all...

Girls never talked to each other about screwing. If you did you were slack. We thought it was a secret between us and our boyfriends. Yet that's all the boys *did* talk about, way out on the flat sea, sitting on their boards, in between sets. They told every detail. The Greenhills guys knew the ins and outs of every girl in the gang.

Monday mornings weren't so bad if I'd done something exciting on the weekend to brag about. The other girls clamoured around me in the morning to hear the latest stories and to see the freshest love bites.

'What time didja get home?'

'Whadja Mum say?'

'Then what did he do?'

And it never stopped. Even when the bell rang, the surfie saga continued.

8

frankly, i'm disgusted

'NOW, who can tell me the adverb in this understated clause? Larkham? Basin?'

'Oh, Mr Fairburn, you haven't told us about your fishing trip yet...'

'Yeah!' chorused the second form English class.

'Oh...ho...you don't want to hear about that.'

'Pleeease, sir,' cried Larkham.

'Ah go on, sir,' whined Basin.

'All right, all right...'

Phew. The class sat back for a bludge. Once we got him going he'd talk away at least half the period.

I scratched out a note to Sue, wrapped it around my rubber and dropped it in the aisle between us.

'Psst.'

Sue, nodding attentively at Mr Fairburn's story, reached down to pull up her sock, scooping up the rubber at the same time. She put it in her lap and read it.

'Sue—Bruce wants me to meet him down the creek this arvo. Don't think I'm slack, but do you reckon I should let him again? I don't want to get a bad name. I don't reckon he really likes me.'

Sue looked at Mr Fairburn, her eyes wide with attention and waited till the teacher cast his imaginary rod out of the window to scribble back a note to me. She put it into her pencil case and passed it across.

'Look Debbie—Kim told me that Bruce's wrapped in ya,' it said. 'Meet him but don't let him use you. Lend us your ruler?'

I smiled at Mr Fairburn encouragingly, and passed another note, under the table and across the aisle. Sue propped it up behind her English book and read it.

'I don't want him to go round with me just for what he can get. I don't want him to think that I'm just a rooting machine. Debbie and Bruce forever.'

There was no more room to write anything. The slip of paper was crammed with scribbled messages and hearts and old maths equations.

The bell went just as Mr Fairburn was hauling in his 'whopper'.

Susan chucked the screwed up note into the bin as we went to meet the gang for lunch.

I did meet Bruce after school. We shared a cigarette and blew smoke rings behind the lantana.

Next afternoon I was daydreaming out of the window, when a messenger from the office came in.

'Deborah,' said Mr Fairburn, 'Deborah Vickers, you're wanted in the headmaster's office immediately.'

I nearly choked. A wave of fear rushed through me. 'What have I done?' I thought. The whole class looked around at me. Was it smoking or nicking off? I couldn't think of anything. The school was deadly quiet as I walked across the quadrangle. The sun glared down on the grey, bare asphalt. Used meat-pie wrappers and lunch bags blew about the bins, and I wished Sue was with me.

I knocked timidly on Mr Bishop's door. His bald head looked up. 'Come in, lassie.'

I entered.

'Take a seat.'

I sat.

He 'ummed' and 'ahhed' and sighed. He rubbed his wrinkled temples and drummed his hairy fingers on the desk.

'I'm disappointed in you, lassie...Frankly, I'm disgusted!' A little bit of spit shot across the table. 'Tch, tch, tch...' For a moment he was overcome.

I clutched the sides of my seat. He opened his desk drawer and pulled out a ragged piece of paper. He waved it in my face. I still didn't know what he was talking about.

'Maybe this will refresh your memory...I-don't-want-him-to-go-round-with-me-just-for-what-he-can-get...I-don't-want-him-to-think-I'm-just-a-*rooting*-machine.' I sat on in agony. 'Don't try to deny it. It was found in the garbage bin by the cleaning woman yesterday. After *your* English class. She did the correct thing and brought it to me and I acted upon it immediately. I know the boy involved. I never expected this of you Deborah. *Rooting machine!* Would you mind elaborating on that?' He leant forward.

I thought quickly. 'Everybody says it, sir. It doesn't mean anything.'

'Am I to assume you've had *sexual intercourse* with that long-haired lout—Bruce Board?' I nearly spewed.

He went on and on. He threatened to keep the note in his safe. He promised to send it to the Director of Education if I stepped out of line between now and when I left school and I wouldn't get my HSC. I wouldn't get a job. My parents would be informed. 'So, Deborah Vickers, you'd better pull your socks up...'

Sue rang me that night.

'Hi, Deb. What happened?'

'He cracked a mental.'

'What for?'

'He found the note.'

'Deadset? Are ya on detention? Is he gonna tell ya olds?'

'Yeah, so he reckons.'

'No bull? What a weak act.'

'Oh the old perv. Bishop can stick it.'

'Anyway, has Bruce rung ya yet?'

'Nah. He rings me at eight.'

'Deadset? Every Wednesday? Jeez, he's roolly stoked in ya Deb. Treats ya roolly good and stuff.'

'Yeah reckon. How 'bout Danny? Does he...tch! Oh hang on, it's me old lady...Wot Mum?...Sue!... Yeah! I gotta ask her a science question don't I?... Righto...'

Being a girl, I never rang Bruce. I just spent all Wednesday night by the phone. That gave me time to write out the junk I was going to say to him.

1. Didja hear about Frieda Cummins?
2. How was the surf?
3. Did you watch Number 96?
4. Got called down to the headmaster's today.
5. What are we doin' Friday night?

His contribution to the conversation consisted of a grunt, 'yeah', 'deadset', 'unroole', 'perf', 'na', 'dunno', and 'seeya'.

'Bruce, what are we doin' Friday night?'

'Danny wantsta go to the drive-in.'

'Who's goin'?'

'I dunno. Deakin. Kim. Me.'

'What's on?'

'I dunno.'

'Okay, pick us up Friday.'

'Righto seeya.'

I hung up the phone. 'Mum...?' She was packing Thursday's lunches in the kitchen.

'Yes dear.'

'Can I go to the pictures with Sue on Friday night?'

'Who else is going?'

'Oh, all the other girls. Kim and Tracey and them.'

'Not "them". The others. Kim and Tracey and the others.'

'Kim and Tracey and the others.'

'What's on?'

'James Bond. It's only rated "M". We're catching the bus and then Mr Knight'll pick us up. Oh, go on.'

'Go ask your father.'

'*Dad…*'

On Friday evening I got ready. I wore straight-legged Levis and see-through underpants.

'Now behave yourself.'

'Yes, Mum.'

'And thank Mr Knight.'

'Yes, Mum.'

'And don't sit near the aisle.'

'Huh?'

'Some pusher may jab you in the arm with Heaven-knows-what. I read about it in the *Mirror.*'

'Yes, Mum.'

Bruce wasn't allowed at my place anymore. I wasn't even supposed to be going out with him. Sue's parents were cool, so I usually met him up there. My mum and dad thought he was 'undesirable'.

'He's got nothing going for him,' my mother said.

'He's below your standard, Deborah.'

'How can you possibly find anything to talk to him about? What do you *do* with the boy all weekend?'

Then my father would pipe up. 'What does his father do for a living?'

'Yes,' my mother would add, 'what kind of house does he live in?'

Bruce's father was a brickie's labourer and they lived in a small fibro house. It was very embarrassing when I first brought him home. We had a three-storeyed red brick house with three bathrooms and a pool.

He had made a bad first impression on my parents.

My father glared at him as he bounced across the new shag-pile carpet, in his sandy, damp thongs.

'Dad. This is Bruce. Bruce, my father.'

'Gidday, Mr Vickers. Gettin' heaps?'

'How do you do?' My father left the room.

'Jeez! This is a fuckin' mansion!' Bruce said, flopping into the newly upholstered Keith Lord lounge suite that no one ever sat on.

'Sssshh…Not so loud.' Swearing was unheard of in my house. My pocket money was fined every time I swore or 'took the Lord's name in vain'.

He ate all the biscuits, swore at my little brother and smoked my father's cigarettes. My mother was weeding the azaleas as I walked him down to the car. She came over to say goodbye, glancing in the back of his hotted-up panel van. She took note of the double mattress and the sex posters on the wall.

Bruce was revved up. 'Seeya later old cheese!' he cried and roared down the driveway.

From then on Bruce always had to pick me up on the corner.

9

his money's worth

IN the smothering darkness, the girls lay side by side.

'What's it like?' Kim asked.

'What's what like?'

'You know.'

'What?'

'Screwing,' she said.

'I don't know.' Sue acted innocently.

'Yes you do, Danny told me.'

'What!'

'It's all right. After all, I *am* his sister.'

Susan blushed hotly in the darkness, and said nothing. Kim wasn't even her best friend.

'I can hardly breathe.'

'Come on, tell me,' Kim demanded. She was terrified.

'Sssssshhh!'

They could hear the muffled voice of the attendant.

'Four adults? Five dollars…'

Once inside the drive-in, Kim and Susan were allowed out from under the panel-van mattress. They were giggling and dishevelled.

'I thought I was going to die!' said Sue, tucking in her shirt. 'I could hardly breathe.'

Kim was brushing her long, thick, brown hair. I was lucky. I was Bruce's girl and got to ride in the front the whole way.

The boys had arranged it beforehand. Susan and Danny got in the back first…that way they only missed out on the beginning of the movie. They were quick and never made a noise. Except sometimes you could hear Danny undoing his belt. Sue lay there, straining to get a glimpse of the movie over his pumping shoulder. They finished before the feature film, *Easy Rider*.

Then there was interval. The boys ate hot chips while the girls smoked cigarettes. Towards the end of the ads, Bruce pulled me over the seat and drew the curtain. It was easy enough taking all my clothes off, but I couldn't always find them again, so I usually left my shoes and socks on.

'Didja bring the vaseline?'

I had the jar tucked up my sleeve. It was an awkward thing to carry around.

'What are you taking that for?' my mother would ask.

'Oh, I've got cracked lips.'

Bruce applied it to me, then saddled his dick with

a rubber frenchie from his 'Tool Kit'. After basting his utensil, it was a series of: 'Ugh...Grunt. Push. Ouch! Ugh! Ugh!'

'Move back,' Bruce complained. 'I'm hittin' me 'ead.'

Edging back, I tried to spread wider. I gritted my teeth and fixed my eyes on a poster on the panel van wall. 'Things to do today,' it said, with two stiff figures copulating in the traditional position.

It never worked, vaseline or no vaseline. It was physically impossible. I was under-developed and thirteen. Bruce was over-developed and seventeen. It seemed hours before he gave up. But it wasn't over yet. Bruce had to get his money's worth, after all he'd paid for me to get into the drive-in.

Next thing I knew I was being smothered by hair, thighs and a determined utensil. I choked, spluttered, sucked, gasped and gulped.

'Watch out for ya teef!' Bruce ordered.

Then it was a fumbling grope for underwear. Buttoning. Zipping. Hooking. Pulling on everything inside out. And at last back to the film.

It was different for Kim and Dave. They liked each other. We all knew they were both virgins and after a few minutes it was quite clear...'Oww! Ooh no. It's hurting. Ouch!' Sob. But you have to keep going.

Danny and Sue and Bruce and I all sat in the front seat watching the film.

'K'niver drag?'

'Aw, righto.'

'Move over, Danny.'

Sue and I glanced nervously at each other and now and then stole glimpses of Danny, Kim's brother. His face remained blank and impartial. The noises in the back grew more frantic as the love scene on the big, white screen climaxed.

A few days later, Bruce stopped ringing me up. This meant I was dropped. Sue confirmed it at school.

'Hey Deb...Bruce told me he doesn't want to go roun' wiv you anymore.'

10

dropped

GETTING drunk was the coolest thing to do. Smoking Marlboro didn't impress anyone anymore. We'd never touched alcohol before, but Tracey and Kim had been drunk three times. So we parted with our precious pocket money and Strack bought the stuff.

That afternoon after school, Sue and I met Steve Strachan in the church yard. We gave him ninety-nine cents each and ordered two bottles of Brandivino.

We could hardly eat our peas for excitement. When Mrs Knight looked the other way, we scraped our mashed potato into the compost bucket.

'What's the time?' I asked.

'We've got to have some milk before we go.'

'Yuk. What for?'

'If you drink it before, you don't spew after.'

'How come?'

'It lines your stomach or something…here yar.'
Sue handed me the milk jug.

That night we roamed Oleander Parade clutching
our bottles, looking for a secluded hiding spot. We
didn't want anybody's mother to see us.

Across the road from our jazz ballet teacher's, we
camped on the strip of cement driveway, between
a Kingswood and a Monaro. We guzzled the stuff,
daring each other on.

Then it was off to the party.

By the time we reached Waratah Street, we
were well and truly plastered. We crawled along the
well-shaven lawns to Number 32—Vicki Russell's
fourteenth birthday party. The whole gang was there;
trying or pretending to be drunk. We staggered into
the centre of the party. They were all watching TV.
Bruce was there too, nursing Kerrie in the armchair.
It freaked me and I ran outside.

Danny found Sue and led her out into the back
room.

'I wanna watch TV. Come on Danny, I wanna
watch TV.' Susan drawled.

Danny laid her down on the old couch. He had
other ideas. Dave Deakin barged in.

'Do up your fly,' Danny whispered, taking charge
of the situation.

'What? What's going on?' Sue murmured into the
cushion.

'Bruce's here and Deb's freakin' out,' Dave said.

'She's pissed. You better get her Danny.'

David and Danny came to find me. I was lying in the driveway, yelling at people as they stepped over me.

'I've got m' rags! I've got m' rags!'

'Shut up! Stop shouting.'

'I've got m' rags Dan!'

I was petrified now that he dropped me, that Bruce would tell all the other guys that I was too young and too tight. I was trying to prove I was grown-up.

In those days, if you were thirteen and didn't have your periods, you weren't grown-up. I didn't have my periods so I wanted everyone at Vicki Russell's party to think I did.

At half past eight, Danny's father drove us home.

Mrs Knight opened the door in her pyjamas.

'I think they're ill,' said Mr Dixon.

We were drunk at seven. We were home in bed by nine. Mrs Knight undressed us and filled us up with soda water. 'Someone put something in our drinks,' we explained. The buckets by our beds soon overflowed. Later that night, in simultaneous moments of agony, we met each other in the bathroom. We took it in turns to spew and then sat on the cold bath tub.

'I feel terrible.'

'So do I.'

'So much for the milk.'

Danny was worried about Sue and me getting a bad name. It was okay for girls to get drunk, but only if they had a boyfriend. Surfies would never touch someone else's chick, but a single drunk girl was an easy lay.

Danny couldn't have his girlfriend associating with a potential moll. So he brought down his best friend—Garry Hennessey. Hen had just broken it off with Vicki 'cause she two-timed. He asked me to go round with him that night. And from there on it was another cute little foursome. We did everything together.

Usually we had nowhere to go. We either hung out at the bowling alley, sneaked into the pub—dressed up and drastically under-aged, or sat around Miranda Fair Shopping Centre—especially on Thursday nights. Everyone went up there. It was just a big, lit-up, out-of-the-rain place where we could all meet. You had to keep your eyes peeled for the security guards though. They'd 'move you on' and chuck you out if you couldn't prove you'd bought something. We would have 'moved-on' gladly, if there'd been anywhere to 'move on' to. We slouched around Grace Brothers Camellia Court all night or hung out at the bus stops out the front. There were heaps of us. The girls checked out the guys and the guys checked out the chicks. Everyone was in their best Levis. Eyelashes freshly mascaraed, hair brushed...

'Goodday Cheryl...how's Wayne?'

'Oh, Hi! Good. Real good. How's Danny?'

'Good. What are you doing up here?'

'Oh…Ar…Oh, I had to get a pair of sandals…
What are *you* doing up here?'

'Oh…Ar…Oh, I had to come up with Debbie to
get her blue angora off lay-by.'

'Oh…'

No one would ever admit that we went up there
'cause there was nothing else to do.

'Guess what?'

'Wot?'

'Guess who I saw lookin' in the window of Angus
and Coote?'

'Who?'

'Danny. I reckon he's gettin' you a ring…'

'Ya never…'

'I deadest did…'

'When?'

'Just then.'

'Oh…he can't be.'

'He *is*! How long's he bin goin' out with ya? Three
months?'

'Three months and two days.'

'Well, 'bout bloody time.'

Getting a friendship ring was the biggest thing in
a girl's life. If you had a ring you were a top chick.
Girls rushed up to you every day at school.

'Give us a look. Oh…Is it eighteen-carat?'

'Yeah, have a look.'

'Oh gee, he treats ya good. It's bewdiful.'

'Yeah, he treats me roolly good and stuff.'

71

'How long have you been goin' round with 'im now?'

'Three months, two weeks, four days and um… what's the time?…two hours.'

'Whenja get it?'

'Saturday night.'

On the way home from your boyfriend's place, just after he'd given you a ring, you'd pause under the street light and examine it. Was it eighteen-carat?… Phew.

By day, we were at school learning logarithms, but by night—in the back of cars, under the bowling alley, on Cronulla Beach, down behind the Ace-of-Spades Hotel, in the changing rooms of the football field, or, if you were lucky, in a bed while someone's parents were out—you paid off your friendship ring.

Cheryl Nolan, one of the top chicks, got a ring every few weeks from a different boy. That's why she was a top chick. She had a horse and was a good screw.

'I think he's gettin' me one,' she said to me.

'How do ya know?'

''Cause Vicki saw him goin' to Miranda Fair, by himself on Thursday night. He must be.'

The guys slouched around in big, blonde groups, up against railings and shop corners. If your boy-friend was there, you didn't hang around him 'cause he was with his mates. You stayed with the girls and walked around on parade, going from the Fashion Wheel Boutique to the Igloo Deli to the Fashion Wheel Boutique to Surf Dive and Ski.

If your boyfriend had just dropped you, it was easy to find someone else up at Miranda Fair. It was a cool game of checking out and chasings.

'Hey Sue…who's that over there?'

'Where?'

'The one with the long blonde hair.'

'He's in Spotty's gang.'

'Hey, walk over with me.'

'Na.'

'Go on! We'll pretend we're lookin' in the record shop.'

'Well, do I look all right?'

'Yeah, check him out will ya? What a doll.'

We sauntered over, casual as hell, with all eyes on us. When there were no boys that we fancied, which was rare 'cause usually we fancied anything with blonde hair and Levis, we bitched about our girlfriends.

'Oh, check out what Vicki's wearing. She saw me up here buyin' me black Californians, so she went out and bought exactly the same thing.'

'Small weak act.'

'Yeah, she's a two-faced bitch.'

'Yeah, 'cause she was going roun' with Garry for two months and he was roolly wrapped in 'er, and she was two-timing him. She had a ring and everything. I dunno what he saw in 'er.'

'God, she needs a new head…oh, gidday Vick. What are you doin' up here?'

The big time was when someone's parents went away for the weekend. We'd then have a whole house to ourselves. Beds. Television. Telephone. Record player. Fridge. Vacuum cleaner. It was just like being in a big doll's house, and that's exactly what we did—play house.

Occasionally Garry Hennessey's parents went to Hawaii or somewhere. Then everyone in Sylvania lived at Garry's place for the weekend. The old gang. Johnno and the boys. There was no one to hassle us and plenty of food money, which Garry spent on beer and cigarettes. The boys sat around drinking, smoking, playing pool and cards.

When they felt especially energetic and the surf was bad, they donned their wetsuits for a quick skin-dive in the sewer canals of Sylvania Waters. After a few hours they retrieved such treasures as rusty refrigerators, mouldy dragsters and their pride and joy—prams. They dragged them back, showed them off and chucked them back in.

Us girls pottered about in the kitchen. We spent three hours making a White Wings packet cake, to get the boys' attention, and it took them three seconds to eat it and forget about us. We were left with crumbs, cracked egg shells and a huge mound of washing up. But we didn't even mind that. We were playing mother.

We bustled them into the bathroom and bathed their injuries. Invisible scratches and tiny bruises were drowned in Dettol and dabbed with Savlon. Cotton wool, Band-aids and layers of crepe bandages made us feel important.

Rainy weather weekends were the best. If the surf was flat and it was freezing cold, the boys didn't go to the beach. Then, for a whole two days we'd have them to ourselves.

One Saturday, after a breakfast of pancakes smothered in sugar and margarine, we raced down to Hen's in the rain. Sue was supposed to be sleeping at my place and I was supposed to be sleeping at Sue's.

This day it was really teeming. As we were running past the fortieth two-storied, red-bricked, imitation Spanish monstrosity, a big, white double garage door growled open.

'*Ey.*' It was Deak's house. 'Debbie and Sue.' We turned around. 'What are yews doin'?'

'Goin' to Hen's,' we bellowed. 'His olds are away.'

Through the pouring rain we could see three blurred, blonde heads hanging out of the garage door. They called us in for a fag. We dripped our way up the driveway. There was Dave, Strack and Johnno.

Because it was raining they were in Dave's dad's garage playing ping-pong and scrounging cigarettes.

After a Marlboro each we hit the road.

'See yas there later,' they called out after us. 'We'll spread the word!'

For the rest of the way we planned how to get the boys' attention once we got there. We'd tried making cakes. We'd tried dancing, singing and the silent treatment. We'd tried everything...the boys kept playing pontoon. There was only one thing left to do...

'Deal us in Danny.'

'K'niver cig Jacko?' I asked, under the strain of the game.

'Rack off.'

'Scab.'

The card table was littered with encrusted plates and cold, half-eaten meat pies.

Sue and I pulled out our pocket money and started laying heavy bets. 'Twenty cents.' We didn't have a clue how to play.

'Hey! Where's me dollar note gorn?' I jumped up in defence.

A dollar was a hundred dollars in those days. The boys smirked; they'd passed it round to Jacko.

'Come on. Who's got it?'

'That's weak. That's really weak,' said Sue, sticking up for me.

'Come on. Give it back. Who's got it?'

Jacko started laughing.

'Jacko!' I whinged, snatching at his wrist. 'Come on Jacko. Stop being weak.' It was no use. Jacko was a scab. I sneaked off to the kitchen.

Returning with a milk bottle, I crept up behind him and dripped three drops of water on his scabby old head. I'd gone too far. In a flash Jacko was up, brandishing a full family-size tomato sauce bottle. It splattered bright red on pale blue. All over my brand new, hot-from-Miranda Fair angora jumper. My jaw dropped. The boys gaped at me in silence I went upstairs to have a shower. It was in my hair and every-thing.

'Now, mind the door,' I stressed to Sue. 'Don't let anyone in.'

Sue kept a foot under the door as I washed the angora jumper. As the tomato sauce went down the drain, we bitched about Jacko. Boy, was he a scab.

'Good head he'd have for sure.'

'Yeah, mint of the brains.'

Downstairs we could hear the boys laying on the heavy.

'Watcha do that for?' said Hen, my boyfriend.

'Pretty weak Jackson.'

'Oh, small scab Jacko.'

'She asked for it but!'

'Oh, and she did for sure,' said the Hen.

I hauled on one of Garry's jumpers.

'Oh, it's so big. The arms keep falling down.' Hee, hee.

'Hey, Debbie,' ventured Jacko, outside the bath-room door.

'Yeah?'

'Wanna fag?'

'Yeah.'

He was forgiven.

We spent the afternoon in the bathroom getting

ready. We plucked away all our eyebrows and shaved the bottom half of our legs.

The boys were out buying the grog and cigarettes for the night.

By nine o'clock the party was raging. The word had got around. Everyone was there. The telephone kept ringing, the record player was booming and the front door kept opening as more and more people poured in and the tide in the liquor cupboard went out. When it got late enough we tried playing real mothers and fathers. Not that it ever worked all that well. Everyone sat around cuddling, kissing and cracking on to each other.

Sue and I were desperate romantics. We were always trying to get the boys to say what they said on *Number 96*...

'It's you! You're the one!'

'Kiss me...Kiss me, darling.' (heavy passionate breathing)

'And when we get older, there'll be just you and me. Forever...Together.'

The most we ever got out of Danny and Garry was an occasional grunt and a friendship ring.

To encourage them a little, I put on our favourite single, 'Tickle Me', by Pat Boone. Everyone else left the room. We were with our boyfriends...alone.

With the help of half a dozen cans of beer, Sue and I induced them to tickle us on the floor.

'Oh! Danny! Don't!'

'Stop it Garry!' Giggle, giggle, giggle.

We writhed and squirmed in delight on the shaggy carpet.

Danny leant down and whispered in Susan's ear. 'Comin' upstairs?'

'Whadaya want?'

'A root.'

'I'll think about it.'

So she thought about it. She rolled over next to the speaker and with Deep Purple blaring down her earhole, she thought about it.

'Comin'?' He led her by the hand up the stairs and into Garry's bedroom.

He undid her black cords. He unbuckled his belt. He lay on top of her, and snorted. She tensed as his hand slid under the elastic of her best underpants. The room was silent. Danny knew two things about making love. Tits here. Cunt there. You make a grab at one, then a dive for the other.

Suddenly it was all too much for her. She collected all her morals and movie lines.

'Is that all you want?' She jumped up, zipping her fly.

'Huh?...Ar...Na.'

I had been lurking around outside in the corridor.

'What happened?' I asked as Sue rushed by.

'Nuthin'.'

'Tell me.'

'I'll tell ya later.'

Garry led me into his room. He turned off the light and we lay on the already dishevelled bed.

'Can I?'

'No. I'm on m' rags.'

I wasn't, but it was a good excuse.

I met Sue in the TV room.

'What happened? asked Sue.

'Nuthin'.'

'Tell me.'

'Nuthin'.' I replied.

'Well, didja?'

'What?'

'Didja let him?'

'Did *you*?' I retorted.

'Na. He only wants me for one thing. He's a user.'

'Oh, he is not. What about the ring?'

'What about *your* ring?'

'Oh look, he roolly loves you. He's stoked in ya. No bull. Kim was tellin' Cheryl the other day that Danny told Dave that he's gettin' ya an engraved bracelet.'

'Oh, deadset?'

'Yeah, deadset.'

'I'd better make up,' Sue softened.

'Yeah. He's rapt in ya.'

'Yeah?'

'Ya gonna let him now?'

'I dunno. I'm sick of it. What if I get pregnant?'

'Ya *won't*. Ya can only get pregnant on the days ya

got ya rags. Trace told me.'

We never thought much about getting pregnant. We didn't know anything about it. We didn't do sex in science till third form. It was too heavy to *really* think about. It just made good gossip when a girl disappeared from school for a few days. 'Don't tell anyone, but Tracey…' It was okay if a top surfie chick had an abortion. She handled it and never talked about it. That made her even cooler. But if a moll had one everybody knew and she was always crying. That made her even slacker.

11

gee, they must really like me

ALL our attempts at romance failed miserably and the only time we ever got close to our boyfriends was when they were on top of us panting. It was hopeless from the beginning, but we kept trying. We lived for those boys. Up till Wednesday of every week, we talked about what we did on the weekend and after Wednesday, talked about what we were going to do the next weekend. Which was exactly the same as the last.

Every home science lesson, Mrs Simmons would be up the front talking about sautéeing onions and washing the glasses first, and all the surfie chicks would be up the very back in a whispering cluster.

'I went down Garry's on Friday night...'

'Yeah? You allowed?'

'Bloody oaff. It's unroole down there. There's a snooker table and a pool...Garry's gunna teach me how to play…' Giggle giggle.

'Yeah. Garry's really good to ya.'

'…and there's a caravan out the back with two beds in it…hee, hee, hee…and we just got so drunk last Sat'dy night on Brandivino.'

'Deadset?'

'Yeah, it was unroole.'

'Wadja Mum say?'

'Nuffin'. She never knew.'

'Yeah, you're really lucky Garry wouldn't take advantage of you in a situation like that.'

'Mmmm…It's his birfday this weekend. Gonna cook him a cake. In a heart shape. Pink, ya reckon?'

'Oh perf…'

'*You* girls up the back! What could you be talking about *now*?'

'Cooking cakes, Miss.'

We all invariably got sent out into the corridor but it didn't matter 'cause we just carried on the conversation out there. That's all we did at school: talk about the weekends. And our weekends meant boys. We talked about them behind our text books in maths. Running around the oval in PE. In a big group on wooden seats at lunchtime. On the way home in the bus. And when you got home, you'd ring up your girlfriend when you were supposed to be doing your geography essay—to talk about them.

'Guess what?'

'What?'

'Didja hear about Trace?'

'Nu.'

'Johnno dropped her.'

'Deadset? Why? They've been goin' round together for heaps.'

'She was two-timin' him last Friday night with Deak.'

'Oh, what a slack-arse. She's gonna get a bad name.'

'Yeah, reckon. Johnno found out and dropped her.'

'Moll.'

The boys could screw as many molls as they liked during the week. No one cared very much about that. We all thought they were dogs. But if any of us girls 'got it off' with another boy, we were immediately dropped. We learnt to fuck just enough not to be called slack or tight.

'What about the ring?'

'She's keepin' it.'

'Oh what a weak act.'

'Yeah reckon. That's what Kim told her. Now Dave wantsa go roun' with her.'

'Deadset? What about Cheryl?'

'Oh, she's gonna crack…Hey don't tell Trace I told ya but.'

'Oh, okay. Didja hear about Frieda Cummins? Small moll…'

'Ssshh, hang on. Mum's coming…Ah…Does rice grow in the Riverina?'

'*What?*'

There were a lot of molls where we grew up. They grovelled around with their pants off under the bowling-alley—in the dark and dirt and spider webs; in the cold, damp caves at Cronulla Beach; in the prickly lantana bushes down the paddock and on the grotty banks of the Georges River behind the Ace of Spades Hotel.

If you were overweight, pimply, a migrant, or just plain ugly, you couldn't get a boyfriend. If you couldn't get a boyfriend, there were two options. You could be a prude or a moll. Being a prude was too boring. If you were a moll, at least people knew who you were. Like Frieda Cummins. She was fat, untanned with red hair and freckles. To make it worse, she was a Pom. Most of her time she spent flat on her back.

Gang bangs usually happened on rainy days, or when the surf was no good. The boys were bored. They weren't seeing their girlfriends till that night. They were restless. All that energy they usually expelled ripping into right-handers and carving into tubes was bottled and bubbling at the brim. Like the day they got Frieda. It was raining. The surf was flat. Nothing much was happening…

'Hey. Check out that chick.'

'Oh…' moaned Johnno, 'Dog-eat-dog.'*

'Hit the brakes, Gull. It's Cummins.'

*Dog-eat-dog—pronounced '*doggy-dooog*' which means a daggy girl—a girl wearing too much make-up, a girl who's too fat or with scraggy hair or just plain ugly.

Slouching down the footpath, in a big grey raincoat, was Frieda Cummins. Johnno wound down the window.

'Eh! Feel like comin', Frieda?'

'Ha, ha, ha, ha…' Wayne jabbed him.

'Shut up,' he whispered. 'Where ya goin', Frieda?'

'Home.'

'Wanna lift?'

She jumped in the car without hesitation. A chance to be with the boys! 'Gee, they must really like me.'

'You gunna drive me home? Yews can come in if ya like.'

'Sure Fried…Just gotta drop in at my place for a minute.'

Back at Seagull's place, Wayne led her off to the bedroom. She couldn't believe it. This was beyond her wildest dreams. Wayne Wright. He was the top surfer. It had taken two months for Cheryl Nolan to get him. Now she was with him, alone…

Outside the boys were fighting over who was going next. Wayne came out. Johnno went in. Followed by Seagull. And then Dave Deakin. And then Jacko. And Danny. Then Boardie. Steve Strachan arrived late.

'I'm not goin' fuckin' slops.'

It didn't matter to Frieda. She couldn't feel it any more. She'd done everything. Maybe now they'd let her in the gang.

Frieda finally staggered out of the bedroom.

'You gunna drive me home now, Gull?'

He sniggered. 'Rack off moll. No fuckin' way.'

She walked through the kitchen, her raincoat still dripping.

'See ya *slut*.' Jacko thumped her hard on the back.

Strack fetched one up his throat, aimed, and a big yellow slag hit the back of her grey raincoat.

The thing is, she always came back for more.

Sometimes the boys had to use more subtle tactics. Like one night down at the pub. There were a few strangers there including one giggly little Bankie chick. The boys thought she looked like an easy lay, so they buttered her up by teaching her how to play pool. She wasn't that easy though. Steve Strachan offered to drive her home to Bankieland. He thought there must be a vacant lot or a deserted alley between Sylvania and Burwood.

'You won't do nuffin', will ya?' she asked. 'Like ya won't take advantage of me?'

They drove off. All the boys were in the back of the panel van.

'I used to be a naughty girl,' she said, 'but I'm not anymore.'

Halfway down the highway, they turned down a dark street.

'Where yas goin'?' she asked, anxiously.

'Stop the car Strack!' demanded Gull, leaning over the front seat. 'Now, get out!'

'What's goin' on?' the girl squeaked.

'Shut ya face or you'll get it too.'

And here's where the play-acting began. Strack got Gull and the rest of the boys to bash him up against the car and act as though they were really punching the shit out of him.

'No!' he shouted, as his head supposedly hit the metal. 'I won't let yas root her!'

They thumped, kicked and bashed the car while Steve made convincing noises. 'Ow!' 'Fuck off!' choke...gasp...groan...

Then she, from inside the van, moved by his heroism, cried, 'Don't hurt him. I'll root yas all. Leave him alone.'

And that was that.

I was down the Alley one day, checking out the guys who were checking out the surf. Skinny Lorraine Peck staggered around the corner. She was pale, and tottering along the footpath. She collapsed outside the milk bar.

I jumped up to go over to her. My boyfriend grabbed me fiercely by the arm. 'Don't get involved.'

'But she's hurt!'

'She's just a fuckin' moll.'

A group of boys gathered around her. The same boys that had 'gone through' her the night before. She lay there moaning, clutching her stomach and writhing on the cement. They nudged and prodded her with their thonged feet.

A moll was just a lump of meat with a hole in it— and that's how they were treated. At least I got a ring.

Friday and Saturday nights the boys went on their milk run. They watched TV until Mrs Dixon went to sleep and then sneaked down to the garage. There they waited for a big truck to come rumbling down the highway and under its noisy camouflage, rolled Danny's mother's Datsun down the driveway. And it was off to Sylvan Headlands at a hundred miles per hour, at three in the morning. Sometimes they picked up Johnno and Dave on the way.

They cruised Sylvania Waters and Sylvan Headlands, the richest areas where some people were foolish enough to leave out two weeks' worth of milk money. They tore up the cheques. The car jingled its way along with heaps of twenty cent pieces.

They didn't' have much to spend their money on. Marijuana wasn't in yet, heroin unheard of, and alcohol an occasional treat when a big brother was obliging. So of an afternoon when we wanted to find the boys we mosied along up to the Arizona Milk Bar. There they'd be, feeding their twenty cent pieces into the pinball machines.

'Give us a game,' we whined.

'Ping off, I'm up to seventeen thousand, five hundred and forty.'

After the boys had a particularly successful haul, they sometimes gave us one of their free games. One flicker each. We always lost, and went back to slouching over the pinball machine, watching them rip.

One night, on the milk run, when all the guys had had a turn at driving, Danny and Greg sneaked the car back into the garage, called Sandy the dog, and headed off for Sue's place. I was staying the night.

Sue and I were fast asleep in our best nighties. We lay cuddled up in Sue's bed. I awoke with a start. There were little drops of cold water all over my face Splat. Splish. I looked up to the window and there were two blond heads peering through the flyscreen. How romantic. They were flicking the slimy fish pond water all over us.

'They're here,' I gasped into Sue's ear.

'Huh?'

'They're here. It's them.'

Sue pulled the blankets over her head.

'The door's open!' I hissed out the window.

They tip-toed in past Mrs Knight's bedroom.

'Come on. Get out,' Danny ordered, nudging me with his foot.

'No. It's too cold,' I whined, clinging on to Sue. Sue lay silent.

'Come on.' He kicked me out of bed. I thumped on to the floor.

Garry and I camped in the corner of the room with the dog.

'I'm freezin',' I complained.

Danny, very generously, chucked over a blanket. Garry and I huddled up on the floor. Danny proceeded to really wreck the bed. Instead of climbing underneath the blankets, he pulled them all out and lay them on top of him. The room was silent, except for the sound of Danny unbuckling and unzipping.

He pulled up Susan's little blue Woolworth's nightie, pulled down her fake, leopard-skin underpants and jabbed it in. Pop. Shove. Pop. Shove. Well, at least Danny would have another mark in Jacko's screwing competition. In Jacko's drawer, pinned to the wood, was a piece of paper with all the boys' names on it. Johnno, Dave, Wayne, Danny, Gull, Hen and Strack. After each conquest they got a tick next to their names. Danny didn't want to come last.

Garry was trying to score.

'Can I?'

'No. I can't. I'm on m' rags.'

Garry was beginning to think I had a 365-day period.

Hours later, I woke up. The sunlight was streaming through the window. I felt stiff and cold and realised I was on the floor. Then I saw Garry. I looked up frantically and there was Danny.

'*Shit!* Garry! Wake up!'

'*Huh?*'

'Danny! Danny! *Danny!*' Boy, he was dense. 'It's morning.' I jumped up and kicked Danny out of bed.

'Huh? What?' groaned Danny, rubbing his eyes.

'Sssh!'

Sue rolled over and pulled the blankets over her head.

'Hurry.' I was madly organising them out the door. 'Hurry.'

'What about me fongs?'

'Look under the blanket...'

Finally they left. Danny yawning and Garry hobbling along beside him.

I crawled into bed with Sue.

'*Bbbrrringgg!*' Mrs Knight's alarm went off in the room next door.

The only way you knew you were someone's girl-friend was because he'd root you every weekend.

It was different for me and Garry. After a while, we really started to like each other. I didn't have to pay off my friendship ring—he gave it to me 'cause we really were friends. We rushed to meet each other at lunchtime, sent each other notes, talked on the phone every night and gave each other birthday presents. The olds just couldn't handle it.

12

i was only talkin' to him

THERE were about fifty people in the canteen line. I rushed up to Sue who was nearly at the serving window.

'Can you get me four cream buns, two salad sandwiches and a Jupiter Bar?'

'Oh all right,' she moaned.

I raced off to meet Garry on the lunch seats. 'Sue's gettin' it for us.' Garry looked over at his best friend Danny, who was gorging a Big Ben meat pie. He was sitting with a garbage bin between his legs to catch the fall-out. As Danny ripped in, big chunks of grey meat oozed out, followed by a stream of blood-red tomato sauce.

'Deadset, I'm starvin',' said Garry drooling.

'Oh, there she is.'

Sue was staggering across the quadrangle, laden

down with cream buns, custard tarts, Coca-Cola and lollies.

'Oh thanks for waitin',' she complained and collapsed on to the bench. 'You owe me two cents Garry.'

For a while there was silence as we tore into our sandwiches.

'Oh deadset, there's no lettuce again.'

A school salad sandwich consisted of two slices of wafer-thin, white bread that soaked up the pink beetroot juice like a sponge. Inside, if you were lucky, you'd get a few stray carrot shavings and a dab of margarine. It was hard to see anything else for the beetroot.

'Well, when am I gunna see ya?' Garry asked me.

'I don't know. Come back to my place.'

'It's too far.'

'Well…whadaya want?' I complained.

'Oh deadset, I'm not gunna walk all the way.'

'Well! Meet me behind the library block then.'

'Okay. Want one?' Garry offered me a eucalyptus ball.

Dodging Mr Berkoff, Sue and I manoeuvred our way back to the second form seats.

That afternoon when the bell rang, I dawdled round behind the library block where Garry was waiting for me.

'Hi.'

'Hi.'

From then on we met there every day after school.

We weren't doing anything but the teachers didn't like it.

About two weeks later I was standing in assembly, scoffing jelly beans. Mr Berkoff was out the front raving on as usual. He pointed at some weedy little first former, 'Get-your-hands-out-of-your-pockets-and-stand-up-straight. I-want-to-see-every-girl-in-white-calf-length-socks-and-every-boy-in-a-tie. Hear-that-Basin? Tracey-Little-second-half-of-lunch-picking-up-paper-duty. Deborah-Vikers-report-to-the-counsellor's-office-at-one-fifteen.'

A black jelly bean wedged itself halfway down my throat. 'Shit,' I hissed to Sue, 'must've been sprung nicking off.' Double science dragged on even longer than usual. For once I didn't muck up. I was too busy being nervous.

The one-fifteen bell rang. Down I went to the counsellor's office, my beetroot sandwich untouched. I stood outside her room, frantically trying to scrape off my pink nail polish. Once inside the office, Mrs Yelland closed the door and attacked.

'I've heard some disturbing news about you, Deborah Vickers.'

I didn't know what I'd done but I was guilty for sure. I imagined expulsion and the Parramatta Girls' Home. Mrs Yelland was known for getting rid of 'undesirables' at school. Sandra Riley had disappeared last term. Mrs Yelland had made her undress to see if she was wearing the regulation underwear. As well as having pink undies on, Sandra had love bites all over her. Mrs Yelland decided Sandra was a bad influence.

'Have you got a boyfriend, Deborah?'

'Yes.'

'And do you like him very much?'

'Yeah.'

'And do you see each other at school every day?'

'Yeah.'

'Then why is it necessary to see him after school?'

She told me I'd made myself Very Conspicuous. She raved on about me being out of bounds and loitering in the school grounds.

'I was only talkin' to him.'

She reminded me that I'd been in trouble before. She didn't know how my mother could approve of me having boyfriends at thirteen. It was 'morally dangerous'. *And* she suspected us of being 'sexual truants'. She said she'd ring my parents about it.

I hadn't been able to eat lunch and now I wouldn't be able to eat tea. The one afternoon I really wanted to see Garry, I had to stand him up and walk home alone. My bag seemed especially heavy as I dodged through the traffic on the highway. It was fuckin' unfair. I stormed home and slammed the door.

'You're home early,' my mother commented from the kitchen.

'So?'

I threw down my bag. Pens and books scattered all over the lounge.

'Has anyone rung?'

'No, dear.'

'What's for tea?' I snarled.

'Chops and peas, dear. All right?'

'Don't we eat anything else round this joint?'

'Deborah!'

I slumped down into a chair near the phone and switched on the telly. I glared at the screen. One *Bewitched*, *The Flintstones*, and *Gilligan's Island* later, I'd wound down.

By the time tea was over and I was finishing my Sara Lee Apricot Danish, I had almost forgotten about Mrs Yelland. I'd stopped jumping every time the phone rang. I even laughed my way through the *Benny Hill Show*. But it all came back to me in bed that night. I couldn't sleep. It just wasn't fair. I hadn't done anything wrong. The pains in my stomach mushroomed. The same pains I'd had in primary school. Doctors had reckoned it was 'appendicitis', 'overeating' or 'growing pains'.

'Mum...Mum...*Mum!*'

'What is it, dear? You going to be sick?'

'Mum, I've got pains.'

'Where?'

'In my stomach. It hurts.'

'Well try to go to sleep, dear.'

'It hurts, Mum...'

'I'll bring you an aspirin. They'll be gone by morning.'

Next day, I slouched over to where the gang was sitting.

'What'd she say?' my girlfriends clamoured around me.

'Didja get detention?'

'Did she yell?'

'Did she ring ya olds?'

Sue offered me a sip of Coke.

'What'd she say?'

'Me and Garry aren't allowed to see each other no more.'

'Oh deadset?'

'Small weak act.'

'How come?'

'Oh she reckons we're sexual truants.'

Kim burst out laughing. 'Jeezus,' she said, 'what a perfect idea!'

My parents never told me if Mrs Yelland rang or not. I was too scared to ask. But I saw Garry more than ever now. Garry meant more to me than anything the olds could do or say. We'd been going round together for three and a half months now. No one knew, but we hadn't rooted. After my vaseline-encrusted, agonising nights with Bruce in the back of the van, I wasn't too anxious to try it again. Because he liked me, Garry didn't hassle me. I'd say no and he'd shut up. But as I didn't want to be a tight-arse, it couldn't go on like this forever.

13

first time

IT was the Christmas holidays. The best time of the year. We got up very early and drove to Palm Beach with Sue's dad and caught the ferry to Currawong— the Knight's annual holiday resort.

Sue and I searched everywhere for boys.

'Who's booked in?' I asked Harry, the cranky old caretaker. 'The Hedges? The Elliots?' They were our Bankie boyfriends from the year before. But no. Just boring old pensioners, fishermen and little kids. Ho hum. We bought our ten-cents worth of lollies. That was our daily bludge from Mr Knight. Sitting on the wharf, munching away on our snakes, jelly babies, cobbers and milk bottles, we discussed our boy-less plight.

'What'll we do?'

'Dunno.'

'We could go over there and check out Palm Beach. There's plenty of guys over there.'

'How do you know?'

'Look!' We scanned the horizon for surfboard-loaded panel vans.

'Maybe we should ring up Danny and Garry.'

'Oh for sure.'

'No, deadset.'

'Who's gunna talk first?'

'You.'

'*You!* It's your idea.'

'What'll I say but?'

'I dunno. Tell 'em there's good surf at Palm Beach.'

We ate a packet of fizzers to get our guts up, got an advance on our lolly money from Sue's dad, and rang Sydney.

'Hello Danny? It's me. Yeah me. What...Yeah. We're here. I miss you...Why don't you come up?... Oh yes you can. Boardie is goin' up the coast. Get a lift wiv 'im. What?...Garry will, he will, he said he would last week...Last Friday, oh go on. It's unreal up here. Please?'

Garry thought he could really score this time...He hitch-hiked up that afternoon in a flash. Danny was coming later.

'Garry!' I rushed up to him. I kissed and hugged him madly.

'Who's this?' asked the caretaker suspiciously.

'Me cousin.'

It was good timing. Sue's dad had to go to Sydney for the night.

'Look after them,' he said to Garry.

Garry nearly dropped dead. '*No worries.*'

After a measly tea of cheese on toast, we bunged the two single beds together and retired early. Sue very discreetly slept on the lounge in the other room.

This was it. I lay in bed, in my orange and white checked nightie with a frill on the bottom, packin' shit.

Garry opened the cupboard door and stood behind it to get undressed. He did a kind of striptease, throwing his clothes over the door…striped T-shirt, straight-legged Levis…I giggled nervously.

He made a dash for the light, whipped off his scungies and dived into bed. He kissed me and climbed aboard.

I was so scared I could hardly open my legs. I thought of the little room. The back of the panel van. The vaseline. I waited for it to happen all over again. I felt it there, hard between my legs. Pressing. Shoving. I squeezed his hips. There was searing pain and then it was in.

He started moving and after a while, so did I. So this is what it was all about. Throbbing and pulsing and rhythm. It broke warm down my legs. He kept kissing me till we both crashed out.

Hours later, 'Susan, *Susan.*' It was Harry the

caretaker…he was flashing his torch through the bedroom window. 'Susan?'

Garry leapt up in his birthday suit and charged into the cupboard. I scrambled out of bed.

'Is that you Susan?'

'Yes.'

'Yews right in there?'

'Yes.'

'Your dad just rang and said I was to check on yews. I'm just comin' in for a minute.'

'Oh…Ah, no…You'd better not…Debbie's asleep. She's not very well. I don't want to wake her up.'

'Oh, all right.' He paused. 'You sure everythin's all right?'

I was crouched down, with my chin resting on the window-sill, trying to conceal my little naked body.

'Yes. Goodnight,' I said, real casual. My feet were freezing off on the icy lino.

As the torch disappeared down the track, Garry emerged from the cupboard.

'Deadset,' he said, crawling into bed.

'Phew.'

Hours later, I awoke again, randy as hell. I had to get my guts up.

'Garry,' I said, poking him in the ribs. '*Garry.*'

'Huh?'

'Are you tired?'

I rolled over on top of him.

'Na.'

I had a sitting-up one. I liked that, 'cause it made my boobs seem bigger. The two beds started sliding apart and we nearly fell down the middle.

The next morning Danny arrived while we were still in our pyjamas. We all mucked round in the bedroom. I was in a great mood. I lay back, laughing and giggling, chucking a lemon spread. Then Sue noticed. She tried to signal me, pointing all over the place.

'Sue, whadaya doin'?'

'Oh, I just saw the ferry out the winda.'

I went for my early morning pee. 'Sue!' I shrieked from the loo. Sue went to the rescue.

'Something's happened.'

'What?'

'Send the boys away.'

'How?'

'I dunno. Tell 'em to go for a swim or something. I've got them.'

'I know.'

The boys pissed off for a swim. Sue and I examined my underpants. They were coated in thick black blood. There was gallons of it. I thought the world had come to an end.

'We'll have to sneak down the shop.'

'Quick, before the boys come back.'

'What'll I get? Modess?'

'Er. No. You don't want to walk around with a big slice of white bread in your pants all day.'

'I can't use Meds. Mum'll *kill* me. Then she'll know I've done it.'

'Don't tell her.'

We scraped up our ten cent pieces and sneaked down to the shop.

'What if Harry's serving?'

'Oh Gord...'

'We could just point at them.'

Luckily Shirley was behind the counter.

'A packet of...Meds please.'

'First time is it dear?'

'*No.*'

'You'll be all right.'

We ran all the way back to the hut, read the pamphlet and popped one in.

There was no hot water so we had to run a cold bath.

'But it says to avoid cold water,' I moaned over the pamphlet.

'Oh well, it's either this or stink.'

We got into the bath together. I proceeded to outline, in intricate detail, the previous night.

'...You're kidding?...Did he? Hee, hee, hee.'

'I can feel it in there,' I interrupted suddenly.

'You can't.'

'I can. It's falling out.'

'Don't be dumb. Go on...What happened next?'

'And then Harry came to the winda...'

'Deadset?'

'Yeah. It was just so embarrassing. Garry had to get in the cupboard.'

Sue had a sudden vision of Garry's albino body, white hair, white eyebrows, white eyelashes…

'But is he black down there?'

'Where?'

'You know, pubes.'

'Nah. Brown.' We giggled.

Then we heard someone snigger. We freaked. Sue and I scrambled out of the bath and dressed. There, sitting outside the bathroom door, was Garry.

'How long have *you* been there?' I asked, acting cool.

The four of us swam, went for bush walks, pushed each other off the wharf, swung on the swings and flirted.

'Come on Danny,' said Sue. 'I'll show ya round.'

They walked off, hand in hand, into the bush.

'It's perf up here Dan…Look, that's the best hut… there's six bedrooms…You get wallabies round there sometimes at night and—'

'Well are you going to?'

'What?'

'Will ya?'

'What?'

'Root for me.' He put his arm round her waist.

'When?'

'When do you wanna?'

'I don't know.'

'But will ya?'

'Yeah.'

'Well come on.'

'Where?'

He pointed to the bushes.

It was broad daylight. They didn't even have a towel. Susan thought of all the sticks prickling her bare bottom and spiders crawling up her legs…

Danny pulled her by the arm.

'Later,' she said.

'Later' was the middle of the night.

Susan's father was back on the scene so it was a crawling out the window job.

'Tap. Tap. Tap.' Danny's blonde head appeared at the bedroom window.

'Tap. Tap.'

There were two in the bed and the little one crawled out.

She slunk over to the window and had a hell of a time climbing out without letting Danny see her underpants.

Sue had stolen the key to the hut next door from Harry. They sneaked into the pitch blackness. They felt their way into the bedroom and on to the bare matterss. They had to be quick, quiet and careful.

Everything was left just as they'd found it…clean and cold.

She climbed back through the window, duty done.

'Where've you bin?' I shot up in bed.

'*Nowhere.*' Sue crawled back into the warmth of the bed.

'Come on. You can tell me. Where'd ja do it?'

Sue rolled over.

'*Ohhh,* I tell you everything,' I whispered to Sue's back.

'I did what you and Garry did, didn't I?'

'Where?...Just then? Tell me? Where's Garry and Danny?'

'On the beach. Shut up. I wanna go to sleep. I'll tell ya tomorrow.'

14

whada we gonna do now?

AS I was turning fourteen, Brandivino went out and marijuana came in. At last, what everyone had been looking for. Something to do every Friday and Saturday night. We spent all our time buying, selling, smoking and searching for the green weed. Our parents' phone bills went up and garden hoses got shorter.

We smoked the dope in a bong. This is a kind of peace pipe made from a milk bottle with two bits of garden hose stuck in the neck. You stuffed one hose with marijuana, lit it, and dragged furiously on the other. Garden hoses all over Sylvania started shrinking. If we didn't bong it, we smoked it in a joint.

A joint was like a bar of gold. It was 'in', it was illegal and none of the nurds at school smoked it. The best thing you could say about someone was that they were 'really out of it'.

'Should've seen Cheryl at Taren Point dance. She was so whacked.'

'Should've seen *me*! I was so out of it, I couldn't hardly walk. I was just sittin' there and they turned them lights on, you know them purple ones? Oh, and it just freaked me.'

'Deadset.'

'Yeah, deadset. Then the fog machine came on. And I roolly freaked out. Strack kept sayin' "What's wrong?" and shakin' me but I couldn't talk…'

'Deadset?'

'Yeah, I roolly freaked. Then Jacko come up, you know Jack?…and he says to me, "Your eyes look ratshit."'

That was the biggest compliment.

'No bull?'

'No bull.'

'Watcha Mum say when you went home?'

'Oh, I walked in, and me eyes were roole blood-shot, and she said, "Wot's that funny smell?" and I jest said it was incense.'

'She believe ya?'

'Yeah, the Stan.* Then she asked me if I wanted a piece of pizza, and I bust out laughin' and I just couldn't stop, and then me father said, "What's she on?" Oh, it was so heavy man, I jest couldn't handle it.'

Smoking dope gave us something to do with the

*Idiot/Dubbo/Bankie type. Short for Stanley.

boys. It was something to share with them. We still sat around on fences and cuddled in cupboards not talking, but at least it turned us on. It made eating, music and fucking better than before.

The gang began to grow up. Now all the boys had cars and some of the girls were at typing school. We bought better clothes, took longer to get ready, had our hair styled and got bigger, browner, broader, blonder boyfriends.

Garry started to change, too. He stopped coming down so often and sometimes forgot to ring me up. When I did see him, he was quiet and far away. I'd hold his hand but he never wanted to kiss or cuddle me. He was looking scraggy, too; *I* had to brush his hair. Mum didn't like him any more and then Dave told me that he wasn't surfing. It wasn't until much later I realised he was scagged-out on heroin.

Wayne Wright had a car and a job. He'd even been in *Tracks* and won surfing competitions. I wanted someone new and he'd been cracking on to me. I sadly added Garry's ring to my collection.

It was Friday afternoon. Double maths, Mr Berkoff was out the front waving his rod and throwing chalk.

'The logarithms of the tangents are equivalent to the Pythagorean theory of A squared plus B squared equals C squared…What was you answer for this Deborah…*Deborah?*'

'Hmm?'

'You're not paying attention.'

'Um.'

'Watch yourself, girlie.'

'Yes, sir.'

'If you don't want to listen you can go outside.'

I crossed my legs and stared at the blackboard and went on daydreaming.

It was almost Friday night. Half an hour to bell time. We were going out tonight. Wayne was picking me up at seven. I didn't know where we were going or what we were doing...but we were going out. My underpants moistened at the idea. I looked at my watch. Twenty-five minutes to go.

'Sue?'

'Mmmm.'

She was doodling Danny's name all over her pencil case.

'Whadaya wearing tonight?'

'I dunno.' She looked up, worried. 'I just haven't got a thing.'

'I'm wearing m' blue bogarts.'

'Ya new ones?'

'Yeah.'

'I don't know what to do...I wore m' Lees last week and m' Californians, you know the ones with the double stitching, well they're in the wash.'

'What about ya green ones?'

'I wore them *last* Friday night.'

'Oh.'

'Listen…Can I borrow your blue angora?…I won't…'

'*Deborah* and *Susan!*' We stiffened. 'Didn't I tell you two last week not to sit together?'

'Ah…No, sir.'

'Don't try to pull the wool over my eyes. Next time I'd like to see you *here*…and you *there!*' He pointed to opposite sides of the room and threw a piece of chalk at us for emphasis. We ducked. It hit Mike Murphy in the eye.

'Oh, *si-ir-ir!*' He shrieked indignantly.

'All eyes to the front.'

Ten minutes to go.

Making out I was doing my trigonometry examples, I wrote and passed a note to Sue.

'You can wear it. Wayne is getting a deal of hash. Got any cigarettes for the bus?' it said.

Brring! At last. Quarter past three. Sue pulled the Marlboro out of her pencil case. A flood of adrenalin shot through her. It was Friday night.

'You're not wearing that old thing are you?' my mother asked me. 'At least give it an iron.'

'Yes, Mum.'

Wayne was coming in ten minutes. I was all ready. I'd washed my hair. Put on my mascara. Shaved my legs. Dabbed a drop of perfume in the crotch of my underpants and rubbed on Cloud Nine cream to soften the skin on my stomach.

'Make sure that boy brings you home not a stroke over midnight.'

'Yes, Mum.'

'And tell him not to go over thirty miles an hour.'

'Yes, Mum.'

'And behave yourself.'

'Yes, Mum.'

We were off at last. Eight of us in the Holden. I was next to Wayne, who was driving, with my hand on his thigh. There was Tracey, Johnno, Kim, Dave, Sue and Danny.

We drove to a vacant lot in Waratah Street.

'Where we goin'?' asked Dave.

'Dunno,' said Johnno.

'We'll blow a joint first.' Wayne turned off the ignition.

Out came the hash from the glove box.

'Anyone got any Drum?'

'Here yar.'

Wayne mixed it on the street directory; burning the hash and breaking it into the tobacco. He rolled a mean joint. 'Give us the matches.'

The Holden was soon filled with sweet-smelling smoke. The joint was passed across the front seat, along the back seat and back into the front seat. We all took three huge drags each and then passed it on. And then another joint would be doing the circuit and another, and another.

'Ey! Don't bogart* it Johnno.' Johnno was a hog.

'Oh, handle it…'

'That's ya fourth hit, man.'

He passed it on. The joints went round in silence.

Two hours later we were still sitting in a vacant lot in Waratah Street.

'Whada we gonna do now?' asked Johnno, breaking the heavy silence.

Wayne lit up his fortieth cigarette. Everyone watched him pull out the ashtray. He looked at Dave and replied, 'I dunno.'

An hour later, Wayne wound down the window, and asked, 'Well, what are we gonna do now?'

Ten minutes later, Tracey squeaked, 'I dunno,' and wound up the window.

'Why don't we blow another joint?' suggested Danny from the smoky depths of the back seat.

And so, we passed the hours, in stoned silence, sucking on one soggy joint after another, gazing out at the beautiful sight of yet another half–built block of red brick home units.

'Whada we gonna do now?' asked Dave, after we'd blown half a deal.

'I got the munchies sumfin' severe,' said Johnno. 'Maybe we should get some eats, eh?'

'Whadaya reckon?' asked Wayne, his hand on the ignition.

*When someone bogarts a joint they take more than their ration which is three drags.

'I dunno.'

'I don't mind.'

'Whatever yews wanna do.'

We drove off to Roberto's Pizza Hut in Caringbah. We all staggered in, bloodshot-eyed, vague, cool and stoned out of our heads, hoping someone would see us.

'Well, whada you gonna get?' asked Dave.

'I dunno…'

'Whataya gonna get?' asked Danny.

'I dunno…'

Kim asked me, 'Are you gonna get anything?'

'I dunno…are you?'

'I dunno…I will if you do…'

'Um…No,' I lied, my stomach growling ferociously, 'I'm not hungry.'

Skinniness was next to godliness.

Danny ordered a thick-shake and a Carbonossi Special. Wayne got a King Prawn De-Luxe, Johnno got Mushroom and Cheese Delight and Dave hogged himself on four double cheeseburgers. We girls smoked cigarettes in silence while the boys ripped in with greasy fingers and dripping mouths. Then it was eleven thirty. Late enough to go home. Wayne pashed me off and I got out of the car. I couldn't wait to run up the driveway and had to relieve myself behind the camellia bush.

'Phew.'

Now! I stood panting before the fridge. Out came

the sponge cake. The vanilla ice cream. The caramel sauce. One on top of the other. After three huge bowlfuls and a Chocolate Monte, I staggered up to bed and crashed.

It was Monday morning, a few minutes before bell time. We girls clamoured around the heater in the maths room, brushing our hair, pulling up our pantyhose, picking off our split ends and gossiping.

'Didja go out on Friday night?' asked Gail, warming her bottom on the heater.

'Yeah! Didn't get home till twelve thirty!'

'No bull? Whatja mum say?'

'Oh nuffin'. Lend us ya brush will ya?'

'Yeah. Wadja do?'

'Wayne had this unroole hash—we just got so stoned.'

'Yeah?'

'Yeah. Ripped. Saw Darren Peters, Jacko, Strack...'

Bbrringg!

'All right girls. Back to your desks. Books out.'

Gail and I sat together. Sue had to sit next to a nurd on the other side of the room.

'Gee, wish I was allowed out...'

'Yeah, it was unroole,' I said, copying down Gail's homework answers. 'Can't wait till next Friday night.'

15

i can feel something

IT was the same old story of getting all dressed up and having nowhere to go. We were one step further than a year ago, because now we had nowhere to go in a car. That's why nearly every young Australian girl gets deflowered in a car. That's the only place there is. At least we knew Dad wouldn't walk in any minute. At least, not many dads...

One night back when we were thirteen, down Panel Van Point, Cronulla—the deflowering capital of southern Sydney—a distraught father made the rounds. He shone his torch into the backs of all the bouncing panel vans searching desperately for his daughter.

It was Sue and Danny's turn in the back, while Bruce and I sat in the front seat, checking out the midnight swells. Suddenly a beam of light revealed all.

Susan squealed, 'It's the pigs!' and groped frantically for her bra.

'Carolyn, is that you? Carolyn?' The light fell full on her face and then flickered away. Bruce parted the purple curtains and cried out after him, 'Fuck off, you old perv!' But he was already inspecting the next parked panel van.

'Phew,' gasped Danny, re-mounting, 'I thought that was the fuzz.'

I always lay in terror in the back of the van, waiting for the police to catch me. They made regular raids on the parked panel vans at Cronulla Point. They hauled the girls out of the back to check how old they were. They'd even caught Sandra Riley one night. They'd taken her down to the police station, rung her parents and then she disappeared to a girl's home in Parramatta.

I kept my shoes and socks on—just in case. Lucky Sue and I never got caught because we were three years under the age of consent.

But there was nowhere for us kids to go. We couldn't go to a friend's place, because we were so stoned and their parents would see us. Besides that, the record player was always in the lounge and the whole family would be in there watching *Homicide* or *Hawaii Five-0*. So we all got stoned and sat around in the car, until we got hungry enough to go and get something to eat. Then we'd go and hang out at the Pizza Hut, Ma Brown's greasy milk bar, or the Arizona.

That's why it was so great when someone's parents

went out. Just to have somewhere to sit around and drink coffee and watch television. Just to have somewhere to listen to music and cuddle up and relax... even though we were always waiting for the headlights to turn into the driveway.

For a while there we all went down to Cheryl's on Saturday nights. Her parents were *always* out. I rang her and used the code:

'Is it off-shore?'

'Off-shore' meant her parents were out and 'on-shore' meant they were home.

There was plenty of food. Lots of music and a pool. We all sat around the lounge watching TV, smoking joints and eating cheese on toast. After the third joint, things got horny. Sue was on Danny's knee in the middle of the armchair, kissing passionately. Cheryl and Gull were stretched out on the lounge, his hand disappearing into her blouse. Wayne and I were lying on the carpet, half under the stereo which was blaring out 'Close to the Edge' by Yes. That was the in record to play when you were stoned before Cheech and Chong came along.

We had the TV on with the sound turned down and the stereo up full blast. When things got horny and uncomfortable enough, you'd disappear with your partner and go to find an empty bedroom. You didn't just get up and leave though. You had to be cool. You waited until the record needed changing or the dog needed letting out or you wanted a glass of water.

While you were out of the room, you'd pretend it suddenly struck you, 'While I'm up, I wouldn't mind a root.'

I'd started to really enjoy sex now. It was the only thing I had to look forward to.

Wayne led me down the stairs, past the pool, and into the rumpus room. He locked the door. We used to start on the floral night-and-day but always ended up on the floor.

'Let's try a backwards one.'

'Er,' I said. If I rolled over he'd see my bare bottom.

'It's great. Dave and Johnno said it's great.'

'Okay…' I rolled over hesitantly. 'But I don't know what to do.'

'It's all right.' He eased cushions under my abdomen. Finally Wayne said, 'I'm done.'

'Okay.' It was about time to go up for another joint.

'Give it to me,' I stretched out my hand.

'What?'

'You know?'

'I haven't got it.'

'Well, I haven't got it.'

'Where can it be?'

'Gord, I dunno.'

'Well, we'll have to look for it.'

Half naked, we started crawling all over the rumpus room floor. Under the night-and-day. Behind the bar. I even looked behind the piano.

'I can't find it,' I whispered, worried.

'Turn on the light.'

Then I couldn't find the light switch. Eventually we stumbled upon a lamp.

'It's just disappeared...You sure you haven't got it?' I was half under the night-and-day, checking and re-checking. I must have lifted up every cushion in that room twenty times. I had horrible visions of Mrs Nolan doing the vacuuming and coming across a soggy, spermy, screwed up plastic thing. I imagined her picking it up and showing it to her husband; then realising what it was and washing her hands.

We had to give it up. It was just nowhere.

It downed on me in the kitchen...

'I can feel something.' Wayne looked at me. I looked at him. He looked back at his cheese toastie. I went to the bathroom. It had been inside the whole time. Things had got so frantic it had fallen off.

'That's the last time I'm using one of those bloody things,' Wayne groaned.

A few weeks later I was pregnant.

I didn't know I was until one morning I felt really sick.

'I feel sick, Mum.'

'Do you want a day in bed, dear?'

'Yeah.'

'Do you want some Vegemite on toast and a cup of tea?'

'Nu.'

'All right. Look after yourself. Bye now.'

She'd just gone out the door when I desperately wanted to do a pee. Then it happened. It all came out like watery, underset jelly. I flushed it away.

There were certain laws in Sylvania Heights about getting pregnant. We had three ways of trying to get rid of it. You could ride your horse bare-back. Cheryl was always galloping Randy, unsaddled, around the football field. You could get Steve Strachan to punch you in the lower stomach. His friends would hold you while he took aim. It never worked. Some chicks were lucky enough to miscarry but usually you had to tell your father. I could *never* have told mine. Thank God I didn't have to. But it scared me enough to tell Sue. I don't know how Tracey and the other top chicks handled it alone. We went to the doctor's together.

I used Wayne's last name, and put my age up. He knew I was lying and treated me like a slut. The chemist knew I was lying, too. He didn't even put the pill packet in a paper bag. Just as he was handing it to me, Mrs Dixon and Auntie Pam walked in. Sue and I ran home and I hid it in the back of my underpants drawer. Even though it was such a hassle, Sue decided to go on the pill, too.

16

deadset molls

THE Greenhills Gang was changing.

Now we went down the beach for different reasons. We didn't go down to check out the guys or bask in the sun—we went down to score.

'Hey Gull, can you get anything?'

'Oh yeah.'

'Wot?'

'Oh Deak knows a guy who's got some unroole hash. Twenty-five bucks a cap.'

Sue and I scraped together twenty-five dollars from advances on pocket money, selling old records and pawning old friendship rings.

A cap is about half an inch long and looks like a penicillin capsule. It's filled with a black, sickly, sweet-smelling, thick, tar-like oil.

We surfie chicks met in the PE changing rooms

during the girls' assembly, for a smoke. We'd all heard Mrs Yelland's 'girls only' lecture a hundred times. '*Would* you girls kindly use the sanitary incinerators provided? Mr Dunstan has been working for us for twelve years and he's never seen anything like it...'

We had better things to do.

'Hey, lock the door Kim. Didja get the alfoil?'

'Yeah, I knocked it off from home science.'

'Give us it.'

I spotted the hash oil on to the alfoil. Rummaging through my bag I found a half-melted, degutted biro. Tracey lit the alfoil from underneath. I positioned my pen over the brown blotch and sucked up the smoke through the plastic straw.

'Give us a hit,' said Sue.

Pretty soon we were all giggling and buzzing.

'Come on, we'd better split.'

Sue and I headed off for English.

'Do my eyes look bloodshot?' Sue grabbed me frantically by the arm.

'Nah...Do mine?'

'Na.'

'Sorry we're late, Miss. Left something in the PE changing rooms.'

We joined our friends up the back.

'Deadset, I'm so out of it,' I confided in Gail. 'Can you smell it?'

We panicked about our bloodshot eyes all period. If the teacher even glanced in our direction we were sure she knew. The lesson was spent with us freaking out and paranoid behind our books.

For most of us marijuana was enough to relieve the boredom but Frieda Cummins, Jeff Basin and Cheryl Nolan needed more—their mother's Mandrax, Valium or an acid trip at four dollars a pill. It made the day go faster and improved their reputations.

'Cheryl's trippin'.'

'Wot on?'

'White Light. Check out the way she's walkin'! She dropped it on the bus this mornin'.'

During Mr Bishop's lecture in assembly, Cheryl began to sway drunkenly.

'And you, lassie!' he boomed down the microphone, 'Can't you hold yourself up?'

Cheryl yawned at him and the headmaster ordered her up to his office, to be 'dealt with' later.

'Go on lassie. *Move!*'

She started to move across the quadrangle, taking painfully small steps. She walked in slow motion, staring defiantly at Mr Bishop.

No one spoke or moved. The first-form kids even stopped gawking at the dogs screwing outside the science block. We all watched Cheryl totter across the front of the quadrangle. She dragged herself up the steps, planted both feet on the top stair and turned to address the assembly. Letting out a loud raspberry, she stabbed the air savagely with an 'up-yours' gesture and turned to continue her trek to the office. The assembly crumbled. We were laughing so loud we didn't even hear Mr Berkoff blowing his whistle. Cheryl was expelled.

Things were getting heavy for my surfie gang. Vicki's mother found a dope deal in her daughter's drawer and rang up to confide in Mrs Dixon. So Kim got grounded and ran away from home. Johnno got busted for smoking hash. Mum freaked when she saw his picture in the local paper. She told me to get some new friends.

Wayne and I didn't go anywhere anymore. We didn't even go to the drive-in. Friday and Saturday nights we hung out on the main street of Cronulla, buying, selling and smoking dope. Sue and I sat with the boys on the steps of the Soul Patterson's chemist. We could all tell the junkies. They spent most of the night buying hamburgers and then spewing them up into the garbage bins. We'd started to suspect a lot of our friends. Hitting up was the new cool thing to do. If you had needle pricks in your arm, you were tough, and top. A lot of people pretended to be heroin addicts.

'Oh look at Lorraine Peck. The bullshit artist.'

'What? Where?' asked Wayne.

'Oh leaning up against the post office. She doesn't hit up you know. She just scratches herself and coughs, the rag. She'd root for a scaffe,'* I told him.

_____
*A smoke of marijuana.

'Yeah,' agreed Wayne. 'She wouldn't get rooted for a scag† though. She's not worth it. No one would waste it on her. Comin' for a smoke?'

'Nah.' I was too stoned to move. Sue and I kept sitting on the cold cement step while Wayne went off to the parking lot with Danny and Gull to blow another number. As I lit up my Marlboro, Sue nudged me urgently.

'Hey Deb, that's not Garry is it?' She pointed across the road to a washed-out figure huddled in the doorway of the shoe shop. From where I was sitting I could see he was pale and thin. His surfie physique had deteriorated into a soggy slouch. He lifted up his blank face and seemed to stare straight through me.

'God…' I gasped. 'It *is* Garry. Let's go. Quick.' We ran down the alley to the beach and stood very close together on the footpath. Leaning against the railing, Sue and I watched the sea surge, swell and smash on the rocks. A thick thread of smoke coiled up into the sky from the Kurnell oil refinery.

'It stinks,' I said, stamping out my cigarette.

'What?'

'Everything.'

Cronulla was getting duller. More and more of our friends were hitting up. Sue and I were sick of sitting in the car with the boys stoned and paranoid. We were

†A hit of heroin.

sick of fetching Chiko rolls. We were sick of sun-bathing and towel-minding while the boys surfed. For once *we* wanted some of the action. So, we bought a board. It was a cut-down Jackson, for ten dollars. We put in five dollars each. It was pretty dinged but we were really proud of it. After a few weeks we got brave enough to take it to the beach.

On Sunday we caught the nine-fifteen train to Cronulla. As usual.

'We gunna do it?'

'Yeah.'

'I'm packin' shit,' said Sue, heaving the board off the train. Sue carried the fin end and I carried the nose.

'Ya Bankie chicks!' someone called out from the Surf Dive and Ski shop.

We went to South Cronulla first. That was Dick-headland anyway. Two more dickheads wouldn't be that conspicuous.

'You sure there's no one here we know?' Sue said, checking out the crowd.

I laughed at her. 'Who do we know who'd hang out here?'

'What if Danny sees me?'

'Oh, too bad.'

I paddled out first. Sue couldn't stop laughing at me slipping off and getting chundered. After we'd both had a few goes, it was time to show off to the boys. We carted the board up the beach past North Cronulla and Wanda. One surfie jaw dropped after another: 'Hey, check out those chicks!' We dragged our battered board round to Greenhills.

All our gang were there 'cause the sets were pumping. They saw us staggering along from a distance.

Seagull laughed gruffly: 'Hah! Whose chicks are they?'

'Dog-eat-dogs,' moaned Johnno.

'Bloody Towners,' sneered Wayne.

Strack was peeling off his wetsuit. 'Check 'em out. Deadset molls.'

Danny went pale as a shot of recognition electrocuted his face.

'Fucken *Jeezus!*' he moaned and buried his head in the sand.

We approached our gang. They gaped at us, horrified.

'Hey Johnno,' I asked, 'lend us ya boardshorts?'

'Watcha want me boardies for?' He scowled.

'To ride our board,' I explained.

'Cut the shit.'

Our gang disowned us. None of our girlfriends said hello. Sue and I surfed all day. I knelt twice. Sue giggled so much she couldn't even make it to shore lying down. We didn't venture very far out. If I did catch a big wave, I just clutched the sides of the board and screamed all the way in. It was unreal fun.

In between surfs, we dried in the sun with our board between us. The guys from our gang walked by on their way to the afternoon swells. Wayne and

Danny completely ignored us. We were dropped. Steve Strachan paused to peer over us in his big, black wetsuit. 'Yews chicks are bent.' He shook his head. 'Fuckin' bent.'

All afternoon we splashed and squealed and nose-dived. When we were exhausted, Sue and I tried to carry the board home up the beach. The wind bashed it against our legs. We climbed the sandhill at Wanda and looked back.

And there were the boys, a mass of black specks way out to sea. The surf had dropped. They sat astride their boards in the grey, flat water; waiting. I knew they'd be talking about their chicks. They always did, way out there when the waves weren't working.

'Hey Deb, let's get a milk shake.'

Sue and I walked off.

epilogue

ALL this happened a long time ago when we were very young. Some of us have turned twenty now and many of us have changed.

Jeff Basin—Heroin habit.

Bruce Board—Labourer in Caringbah. Unmarried father.

Frieda Cummins—Unknown.

Dave Deakin—Dead. Heroin overdose in Queensland.

Danny Dixon—Plumber in steady job in Sylvania Heights.

Kim Dixon—Numerous breakdowns.

Garry Hennessy—Heroin habit. Serving seven-year gaol sentence for armed robbery of a chemist.

Glen Jackson—Heroin habit. Involved in same robbery but got off. Dobbed Garry and Johnno. Father to Vicki Russell's baby.

Johnno—Heroin habit. Serving nine-year gaol sentence for same robbery.

Tracey Little—Heroin addict, admitted to Drug Rehabilitation Centre.

Kerrie Mead—Fell pregnant, baby adopted.

Cheryl Nolan—Heroin addict, admitted to Drug Rehabilitation Centre.

Darren Peters—Heroin addict, whereabouts unknown.

Vicki Russell—Unmarried mother.

Seagull—Heroin habit and on the run.

Steve Strachan—Gave up surfing and started drinking. Hangs at local pub.

Wayne Wright—Dead. Mysterious heroin-related accident.

Susan Knight and Deborah Vickers—Ran away from school and at eighteen wrote this book.